I0564059

TIME

BREAK

EXPEDITION

THE RETURN

DEAD ADRENALINE

II

Written By Clinton J. Kurtyka

Time Break Expedition The Return, Dead Adrenaline II was written by Clinton J. Kurtyka. The novel, Dead Adrenaline II was completed in the year 2024. All Written, Photographed, and or illustrated material, in whole or in part heron is the sole property of Clinton J. Kurtyka.

Clinton J. Kurtyka is solely responsible for the printing layout and formatting of this material.

Distribution of this text or audio version, and material herein including but not limited to text, audio version, photographs and/ or illustrations by photoplay or copy in whole or in part without prior written consent from Clinton J. Kurtyka is strictly forbidden and prohibited by international law.

Some Images contained herein, are AI generated.

Some the AI generated images have been slightly modified by Clinton. J. Kurtyka.

This is a work of fiction; therefore, the novel's story and characters are fictitious. Any public agencies, institutions, or historical figures, businesses mentioned in the story serve as a backdrop to the characters and their actions, which are wholly imaginary.

The following is a work of fiction, Names, characters, places, businesses, events and incidents are either the product of the author's imagination or used in an entirely fictitious manner. Any resemblance to actual persons, living, dead or semi dead with a Dead Adrenaline virus is entirely coincidental.

Copyright © 2024 by Clinton J. Kurtyka

All rights reserved

Publisher: Clinton J. Kurtyka / Yosai Publishing

ISBN: 979-8-9904588-0-2   (Paperback)

ISBN: 979-8-9904588-1-9   (Digital)

Brief quotations from this book may be allowable with special permission, provided that the accurate acknowledgment of the source is made. Requests for permission for extended quotation from or reproduction of this manuscript in whole or in any part may be granted with permission obtained from the author.

Author Clinton J. Kurtyka picks the action up right where he left off, and you are transported back into the fast-paced action of the world of Dead Adrenaline! Switching timelines and adding new faces, the author puts the foot on the gas and the hits keep coming. The author cleverly mixes science with science fiction, and the bounces between the past and the present are as exhilarating as all the action sequences! The pictures that author has added really help the reader navigate through this strange new world. Join the Man Called Clint and the team as they explore and fight their way through this futuristic zombie apocalypse to a super surprise ending you won't see coming! I thoroughly enjoyed this book and cannot wait for the next one.

Grant A. Miller, author, Murder at Witches' Hollow

Content

Dead Adrenaline

The silence of pain and suffering has awakened.

You cannot hide or step aside, because you have made the choice.

The choice to battle on, until the dawn of a new light.

The line has been drawn in the blood sand; Dead Adrenaline is at hand.

Keep your compass and find a way to rise up and fight another day.

By Clinton J. Kurtyka

Dedication

"This Book is dedicated to **GOD**, Family, Friends and the American way, which matters the most. The rest is most definitely just a **Bullshit** Sandwich."

Prologue

The Year is 2086, political and civil unrest is surfacing throughout the planet Earth. Unrelenting signs of pain and suffering are manifesting within the human population of the world. Quarantined areas are being established to help control the spread of this alien invasion, and for whatever reason these entity organisms have evolved, and are far more aggressive and intelligent than before. Almost as if these savage entities are taking time to plan every attack. Humankind must be like a Yosai Dai (Large Fortress). The human species must have the fortitude to hang on till dawn's early light. The Land of the five governments is fracturing within each sector. The Man called Clint must control the narrative of events and forge an indomitable spirit of men and women with sharpened skills. A force of Burendo Shotokan Warriors must be created in a very short timeline, they must be sent back to the year 2026, and change the past to control the present and future. Will this be done in time for the salvation of human beings? The battlefield arena of contention has been set. **This is that story. One Man's crusade to save planet Earth with a set of fighting skills, weapons of choice, political views, humor, nostalgia, love for family, friends and God, along with a special force of trained Burendo Shotokan Warriors. Let the battle for humanity continue and may our destiny be true.**

Acknowledgment

This acknowledgment goes out to all of the *Storytellers* on this planet, and others. Keep putting your thoughts on the pages, the story will unfold and open like a present on Christmas morning. Give your gift of writing, because someone will read it, even if they're from another planet.

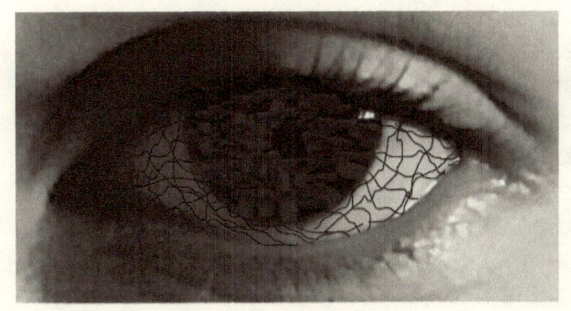

Look For The Signs

Year 2026

"The sound of birds tweeting suffering, and happiness. Blood-coated feathers, and solid red eyes of a gang of birds waiting as spasmodic movements materialize. A fast-moving hiker dressed in what appears to be a futuristic combat Keikogi(Traditional Karate Uniform) is running in a frantic state, deep in the Western Pennsylvania woods of planet Earth. Nature is beautiful. Nature is relaxing. Nature is violent and deadly! The hiker feels the first peck of skin from his neckline. A slight sting of misunderstood movement travels through his body. Then it begins, like a swarm of carnivorous birds stabbing bladed beaks, with every tear of flesh the hiker's agony increases. His flesh begins to fall off, like pine needles from a Pennsylvania Christmas tree. No gifts will be under the Christmas tree this year, only death. The hunger for eradication is unconquerable. Without warning the hiker's shredded body crumbles to the forest floor. Within the blood-soaked remains is a gold embroidered cross sluggishly disappearing into this blood bog of suffering. No last rites, no blessing. Nature is beautiful. Nature is relaxing.

Nature is violent and deadly! The sound of suffering and happiness changes to a symphony of pure happiness. With every wing flap of the gang of birds, blood scabs, tears and liquid splatter throughout the tree line and vegetation floor. The forest begins to transform into a bloodstained open wound. Then, just like a shot from hell's gun it began.

The carnage ends, and the infected cannibalistic birds fly to their above-ground tomb. The alien infection cannot survive in such a weak host. An uncountable number of dead birds cover the forest carpet. Some are piled up like a mountain of flesh, and others are scattered about like a violent nightmare. Nature is beautiful. Nature is relaxing. Nature is violent and deadly. Look for the signs!"

Assembling Warriors

Year 2086

Sensei's log, Throwing star-date 2086, three days from "Time Break Expedition" launch. The infection is spreading but in a more selective direction. Future humans are accumulating in sickbay, due to massive injuries from DA attacks. Many have perished from blood infections caused by DA bites. Irish Warrior from the year 2026 was correct in his deduction that a bite from a DA will eventually kill you by way of blood poisoning. For some unexplained reason, the majority of humans are in a catatonic state but have not changed into cannibalistic savages as of yet. Only a minority of humans have changed into savage beasts on a higher level of viciousness and evilness than before. As this chaos is growing, I'm working lightning fast on establishing "Burendo Shotokan Warriors" for the Time Break Expedition. Hope for humanity is in my hands. Sensei log, signing off.

"I hope you're not signing off Clint, because the world needs you just like biscuits, need extra gravy."

Good one, Austin Maximilian, I Like your style of conversation.

Austin Maximillian

"Why thank you kind sir, but I must say Irish Warrior was completely right. The Man called Clint definitely talks to himself, and sometimes whoever is in earshot of him, will get a great listening experience."

What can I say? It keeps me going Austin.

"Anyways, I'm as concerned as a Prairie Dog looking to the sky for a bird of prey."

Yes, but maybe the Prairie Dog bites back, and doesn't run, and hide this time Austin.

"Yessiree! Let's keep the faith and hope to win the day Clint. By the way, how is the training going with the new recruits for the Time Break Expedition."

Well, let's just say, I have weeded out the dill weeds, and throat kicks really work. You see, one thing your future fighters continue on a path to is sports fighting. The evolution from the year 2026 until now (2086) has contaminated the well of ancient martial arts training. This means too much sport fighting conditioning has disrupted in pure no rules combat. I have quickly disconnected the muscle memory, which causes each fighter not to take advantage. Now each Burendo Shotokan Warrior is striking, kicking, throwing and grappling without a mindset for rules. It took some doing, but after the first couple of painful lessons, these men and women are changing their mindset.

"Well, that sounds better than butterscotch rum over ice cream. On a curious note. How many will be making the trip to the year 2026 Clint."

I have assembled a team of 6 Burendo Shotokan Warriors, along with myself. A maximum of seven are allowed to be sent at one time to the past. Each of them has passed the tesuto (test) and will be a valuable asset to this mission. Along with their fighting skill, they each bring a specialized knowledge that will increase our chances for success. Also, each Warrior is geared up in bite-proof combat field uniforms that should protect a person from a random bite, but these DA(s) may have different (PSI) Pounds Per Square inch of bite power. For instance, an average non-infected human has a bite power of 120-160 PSI. Some of the bite tests of a DA(s) we caught indicated ranges from 400-1000 PSI. Similar to a Wolves bite. Information and research obtained show that the 1000 PSI usually occurs when a DA is in full attack mode. Similar to Canada's Mackenzie River Valley Wolf, which happens to be the deadliest wolf known in the world. This is only the best guess on bite power for these DA(s). Factors like grabbing and tearing human flesh with their DA teeth haven't been tested totally. Just not enough time to complete it. Trust me, we have seen these DA(s) devour humans like piranhas at the dinner table. Two things my warriors must do, first don't get bitten, and second, if they do, don't get bitten in the same spot, or puncturing of the bite-proof combat uniform is possible. Also, a protective helmet type headgear is optional. The reason for this is the headgear tested out did cause optical issues, which made it harder to land a kill shot on a DA.

We don't have enough time to work through this problem, so it is what it is. None of the warriors elected to wear, which I agree with, because our eyes are the best sense we have, so let's not block our view in any way. Plus, each Burendo Warrior has great ability to block headshots, including a violent bite from a DA, which I made sure of. I personally believe this bite proof combat uniform may help some, but if a DA gets into full blood curdling attack mode. No bite proof bullshit is going to work, only pure ass kicking that leads to the death of a DA will totally get the job done. Ok, enough said about that.

On another positive note, an insignia / symbol of each Burendo Warrior specialized skill is embroidered on the right shoulder of each uniform, just to add a coolness factor. Plus, if combat shit hits our land of the living and the DA dead show up. It will be a quick reference to know which Warrior is an expert in what field of knowledge. Trust me when I say this, Austin. A person's mind can weaken in the terminal realm, so keeping it simple will make it easier, plus we don't know if this time travel thing causes memory issues. Also, with the DA storm waiting in the year 2026, and with the one getting ready to erupt in this year of 2086. Things will become one hell of a dill-weed sandwich if you know what I mean.

"I do, Sir Clint of Beaver County, PA."

What are you doing Austin, making up more titles for me.

"Most absolutely Sensei Clint, it keeps me going."

Now you're catching on to my secret Austin. Even in the most devastating consequences, a man must always find peace, humor, nostalgia and a way back to sanity.

Speaking of the word embroidered, which isn't a word used often, especially in the year 2086. It makes nostalgia kick in, and I start thinking of past events in my life. Even something as simple as this. You see, embroidered symbolism reminds me of the business Victorias Embroidering that was located in Rochester, in Beaver County, PA back in the year 2026. I used to get my Belt rank Dan(s)stitched on as I progressed through my Burendo Shotokan higher stages of training. This would only occur if my skill level in my Martial Art of choice upgraded to what Master G required of me or himself for that matter. Fantastic training on a high caliber of defense and attack. Too bad we couldn't have the Victoria's Embroidering place this skill set symbol on our warrior uniform then we would definitely know it would hold up in battle.

I have known the owners for many, many years. Great people, great workmanship. Not sure if they survived when the DA(s) came to town back in the year 2026. Enough said about this, time to move forward, which happens to be traveling to the past. What the hell, speaking of the past, let's see if I can visualize one of the logos the owners created for the business, and the building itself. If memory serves, they didn't have a sign up yet, due to updates to this fine establishment.

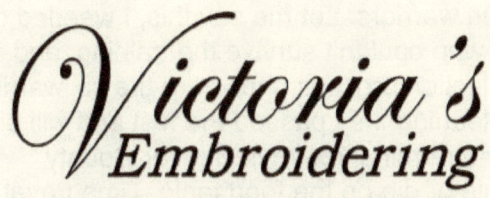

Victoria's Embroidering

Embroidery & Screen Printing

464 Deer Lane, Rochester, PA 15074

724-728-3484

"I know Clint, reminiscing about the past helps a person move forward in the future. Kinda like this morning, I ate a fully loaded breakfast of eggs, bacon, shredded hash browns with some rye toast. Boy was it Chuck-wagon tasty, but I ate it in the past and it showed in the future. Major digestive issues in the future went down."

Yeah Austin, you are a wise man, but you fell completely off the Chuck-wagon with that comparison. Nostalgia brings positive enlightenment feelings into a person's mind, not digestive issues.

"Sorry Clint, a delicious Breakfast keeps me going. Lol."

I see that, Austin; OK let's go down the list of Burendo Shotokan Warriors and skill set bio. I will explain the reason for the optic contact lens feed after I talk about these unique warriors. Let me say this, I weeded out candidates who couldn't survive the training, and after a rigorous selection process, these are the six warriors that were left. Meaning they passed the test and will either survive in the terminal realm in Beaver County Pennsylvania or die on the food table. Time travel to the past will tell the tale, which will be survival or death. If they react, listen, learn, survive, remember and never forget, then they have a good chance of helping this mission go the distance.

Sorry, I got a little sidetracked, but they all know this is a mission into the blade of the Grim Reaper, but each one of them is still on board for this battle.

First on deck will be Logan, along with his aggressive fighting skills. He brings experience in the realm of all branches of anatomy and physiology, including foreign organisms in the human body, which might help us figure out what makes these DA(s) tick. The Human body symbol is embroidered on the right shoulder of his combat uniform, which dictates his master level in both the human structure and the function of these structures. An emerald-colored optic contact lens is placed in his dominant eye.

Logan

Height: 6'1" Weight: 200 lbs.

Second is Olivia, who is an expert in wound care and is a Master level Doctor, which will definitely be useful in the terminal realm. Also, Olivia is one of my top fighters and will end you with the precision of a surgeon. The Caduceus symbol is embroidered on the right shoulder of her combat uniform, which indicates promoting healing and medical care. A coral-colored optic contact lens is placed in her dominant eye.

Olivia

Height: 5'6" Weight: 120 lbs.

Third is Sullivan, he is a lead scientist on this mission, and he will play a significant part in figuring out the science behind this science fiction bullshit sandwich. Plus, he has become very effective in no-rules fighting. An embroidered Atom symbol is on the right shoulder of his combat uniform, which indicates the physics behind this science. A silver-colored optic contact lens is placed in his dominant eye.

Sullivan

Height: 5'10" Weight: 225 lbs.

Fourth is Oliver, who is a Master mathematician and has been part of the top-level involvement in the "Time Break Expedition." On the other hand, don't let his meek personality and size fool you. He is deadly and will take every advantage to eliminate you. An embroidered shield symbol is on the right shoulder of his combat uniform, which indicates his geometry knowledge on a high level. A bronze-colored optic contact lens in his dominant eye.

Oliver

Height: 5'7" Weight: 165 lbs.

Fifth is Silas, he brings the religious grit needed for all to keep the faith. He is our religious balance and has Master level knowledge in each religion our Burendo Warriors may practice. Silas himself is Christian based within his religious beliefs. On the flip side, unlike the greatness of Jesus, Silas will not turn the other cheek and will fight to the death. A Gold Holy Cross symbol is embroidered on the right shoulder of his combat uniform, which indicates the victory of Christ. A gold-colored optic lens in his dominant eye.

Silas

Height: 5'11". Weight: 190 lbs.

Lastly, there is Sandra. She is a top-notch survivalist and can live off the land during any season. Also, her fast reflexes, and uncanny ability for target placement, make her unstoppable when looking for a kill shot. A wilderness mountain top is embroidered indicating her strength in survival. A pearl-colored optic lens is in her dominant eye.

Sandra

Height: 5'8". Weight: 130 lbs.

Another definite bonus these warriors have is that every person on the team has sufficient knowledge to help each other in their specialized field. Also, equipment for each Warrior will be brought to assist with their specialized areas of expertise. Additionally, each "Burendo Shotokan Warrior" is equipped with a "Han'i Ha", which is the weapon of choice. Three ranges of blade use, which is perfect for killing Alien-Zombie organisms. As you know Austin, this weapon was designed by the Irish Warrior and is a technology masterpiece. In fact, so excellent that in this year of 2086, not a single thing was changed or modified. If you see this weapon, it is like three individual weapons all wrapped up in one, depending on what blade range it is set at, it will become that individual weapon. Futuristic style weapon from the year 2026, man Irish Warrior was ahead of his time. In conclusion, each of our warriors has been issued throwing stars and knives, along with a combat ax for close-or long-range accuracy. Common battle weapons, but very dangerous in a well-trained Burendo Shotokan Warrior hand. On a more ninja like thought process, the throwing star isn't your usual suspect for most people, but in my world it is.

"Sounds like your more prepared than me getting ready to eat some waffles and chicken on a Sunday morning in the year 2086."

No shit, they still have that strange combination of food in this future year of 2086.

"Yes Siree, it's one of my favorites believe or not."

Oh, I believe it, based on looking at your waistline.

Anyways, we are ready, but we must be very accurate with our mission, and must make the least number of mistakes we can. It is the unknown obstacles we may face that will give us a life and death run for our money. I have faith in my team and our ability to work through all the pain and suffering we encounter.

"HAN'I HA"

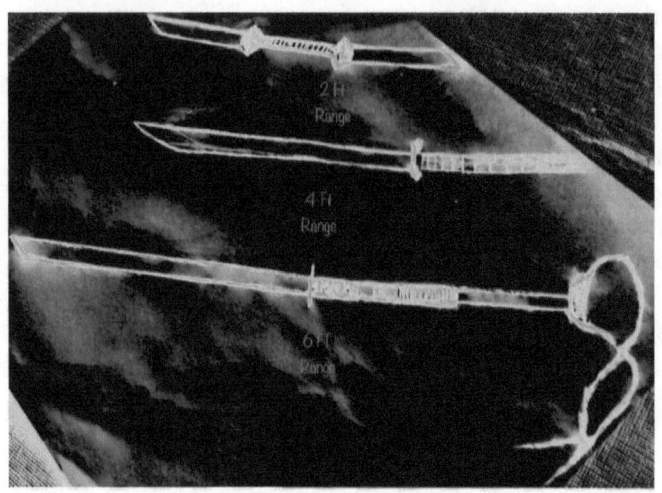

"You are more accurate than a bullseye on an antelope's ass, a Texas Pronghorn antelope to be exact Clint. I must say, this is one magnificent deadly lineup if I do say so myself Clint." Also, with the team leader being "The Man Called Clint," the world knows about you and your credentials. Humanity might move back up to the top of the food chain and get off that Texas picnic table. the way, what symbol will you have on your field combat uniform."

Funny, you asked Austin. Ok, I will have the word 先生 (Sensei) embroidered on my right shoulder, which indicates that I am a leader / teacher. I will guide my Burendo Shotokan Warriors to be their very best. Also, I will have an embroidered patch for One Strike Karate on my left shoulder. As you know I ran this dojo back in the year 2026, each of my Burendo Shotokan Warriors will have the same patch on their left shoulder. They are now officially members of this rare and elite dojo.

"Clint, I love it, a past warrior blending with future warriors. I must say, this is the evolution of the fighting arts. The magnificent seven Burendo Shotokan Warriors have arrived, and you are the leader of the pack!

Well, someone has to be the Alpha, and I'm built for the job.

The Man Called Clint

Height: 6' Weight:200 lbs.

Austin, you crack me up, but you are so right about being Magnificent. Throw me in the mix, and the team is Seven strong. Kinda reminds me of the 1960 American western, *The Magnificent Seven. Starring Yul Brynner, Steve McQueen, James Coburn, Charles Bronson, Robert Vaugh, Brad Dexter, Horst Buchholz. Total of seven gunfighters,* although this western was a remake of Akira Kurosawa's 1954 Japanese film *Seven Samurai.* We are most definitely Seven Samurai(s), plus, guns don't work in DA town, but weapons of choice do.

"Arguing with that Clint, would be like trying to dance with a Texas tornado." Yessiree your team is Magnificent!"

I have to ask you Austin, why is it with all the leaders, military, scientist and other high-level people of the future? You seemed to be dead center in the middle of this shit sandwich. Hell, you were the poor soul that had to convince an entire world nation that my journal was the real deal. This took a lot of doing based on some of the straight dill-weeds in the audience.

"Well now that you've asked this compelling question. You see Clint, I wasn't picked to go to the terminal realm in Beaver County, PA. on that cold December day, two days before Christmas. I volunteered for the right reasons to go on this quest for knowledge.

The Recon salvage unit that had located the journal that day contacted me, and the wagon wheels were set in motion. The leaders and military were behind me, but part of me knew they wanted me to fail. So I went for the right reason, but unfortunately, I was gambling with my reputation and could have been very easily banished from the Hall of Knowledge by Sebastian, the leader of Sector 2. If he would have got the votes, my decision to volunteer would have been for the wrong reasons if I had failed."

Hell, poor Liz Granite was recruited to read the Journal of existence you wrote. Thank Heavens, she went for a throat kick, and sold it to the audience, who were digesting it like a potato pancake of goodness, and they started to believe. Although Cool Blue and you showing up sealed the cork on the old-style Texas whiskey bottle. See Clint, my past, present and future friend. If the wagon wheel comes off the earth's wagon, and the mission isn't a success, they will be coming for me, and I will be the scapegoat. Now I am just a figurehead to showboat around, to bring the world confidence in this Time Break Expedition. Although with

30

the infection seeping like molasses from a tree around us. I might be the last thing on their minds, either way, you must succeed, and stop the crumbling of humanity. "

Wow, Austin, I'm going to say a similar thing I said to Irish Warrior when his ticket was starting to get punched, and he only had a couple of hours to live. Thanks for the vote of confidence, but you just motivated the hell out of me to prove you wrong. Well in this case, prove the world wrong, and slay these alien asshole organisms for good.

"Indeed Clint, yes indeed."

"On a more emotional note, Clint, I do believe you made the correct choice. In reference to not archiving and searching the location of your immediate family, such as your wife (Kim), daughter (Chloe) and son (Luke) in the year 2086. Your son and daughter could still be alive, along with your wife. I believe it's been 60 years since the year 2026, so medical medicine in the area of longevity has evolved in a positive fashion that would amaze you. Out of my curiosity for knowledge what is your last name, Clint?"

My last name you ask. It's a good one Austin. You see, as I have said before, my parents named me Clint after the actor/ director Clint Eastwood. As crazy as it sounds, my last name just so happens to be Westwood. Yep, Clint Westwood, I come from a County in Western Pennsylvania and I make sure Alien ass-kicking happens with real kicks if you know what I mean.

"Clint Westwood, what a cool name for a good futuristic movie or book. Thanks for sharing your last name, Clint. Our life catalog system could locate your family, and whereabouts through DNA, and name location. As I have said before, our medical astonishments in the area of life longevity have increased to a point where people can live a healthy happy life well into 100 years of age. In fact, we do have on our life longevity record over 1 million human beings alive at age 120. Our population in the year 2086 is 400 million roughly and growing, so our human knowledge of longevity is growing faster than the Man called Clint's round house kicks. You say the word Clint, and I will locate your family faster than you can say Texas pecan pie five times."

Yeah, Austin, I would love to see them, but my mind must be clear for the battle ahead. Also, it is better not to disturb the future any more than I already have. Although if I were a betting man, my wife Kim probably figured out I'm "The Man Called Clint" that this future world has been talking about. Let's see, she would be 114 years old. My daughter would be 76 years old, and my son would be 73. Wow, crazy when I attempt to think about it. Yep, leave it up to **God** to know.

"Heaven and earth will pass away, but my words will never pass away. "No one knows about that day or hour, not even the angels in heaven, nor the Son, but only the Father." (Matthew 24:32-36).

Chalice Of Total Decimation

Year 2086

Anyways, I spoke with Gordon Scott, your expert in
wormholes and time travel stuff. He told me that the
mission is on course, and they are ready to launch. I guess
the date of the "Time Break Expedition" is two days from
now. Also, he informed me that my main man Cool Blue
will be making the trip also, and let's just say Cool Blue has
got an upgrade. Believe it or not, Blue can now fly without
the aid of a drone, and has a Chameleon mode, which
gives this robot the ability to blend in with his environment.
Also, the colored optic lenses mentioned earlier in the
Warrior lineup are connected back to Blue. Each Burendo
Shotokan Warrior has a type of contact lens, which will get
direct feed from Cool Blue, so we are all on the same
page. We see what Cool Blue sees. My lens is still a cool
blue color or Aqua Blue. The Burendo Shotokan Warriors
each have their individual lens color as mentioned in their
skill set bio, this optic lens will give all of us the ability to
communicate through optics and audio when needed. I
guess we are now the magnificent 8. That being said, Cool
Blue isn't a living organism, so he can ride with me in the
Time Break Pod, which works for me.

According to Gordon Scott, Blue has some type of
controlled anti-gravity system that gives this android the
ability to fly, along with other cool gadgets. Anyways, in just
two days my team will be going hunting and kill shot time
will begin. On a fun side note, if I were drawing Cool Blue
now, with his bad-ass upgrades, the coolness chalice
would overflow. Let's compare Cool Blue from the past to
the present day.

"Ok Clint, I will humor you with this comical fun,
interestingly different way of looking at life and things. I

must admit, you might be onto something with your way of thinking. Amid this carnival of death circling us in the year 2086, which manifested back in the year 2026. You manage to still find humor and fun in the smallest and unique places."

Yes, I do Austin, so take a quick second and use that low-budget AI machine your future people created, and have it draw Cool Blue, just as I would if I were drawing it by hand. One of Cool Blue from the past and one present.

"Ok Clint, I will scan your thoughts of both the new and old Cool Blue, and the AI machine will do the rest."

Scan away Austin and let's see what the AI machine comes up with.

Nice, yep it is spot on with what I was thinking about how they compared from past to present. I bet this would make a great board game / futuristic AI game of sorts.

. "Funny you said that Clint, because this was from an AI futuristic game called "Match Your Thought." In fact, I was using a portion of the game, so your thought drawings could be created. Older game technology, but still works. Plus, I'm not going to use our high-tech AI for this."

(Cool Blue: Past)

2026

(Cool Blue: Future)

2086

Sorry Austin, I got a little sidetracked with thoughts of Cool Blue drawings, but the upgrades are a bonus for our team and will be very useful during this DA town voyage.

"I expect nothing less from the Man called Clint, it keeps you in a place of calmness and nostalgia. On the flip side of this potato pancake, this mission echoes the chances of prospecting for gold, you might strike it rich or die trying. You see, the richest to be found on these quests will be saving the soul of humanity no matter the cost. Sounds like a double barrel shotgun, with Bujo buckshot loaded in it, waiting for the trigger to be pulled. Hopefully humanity pulls the trigger, and not these invaders from another planet."

Yeah, good old headless Bujo buck from the year 2026, definitely one violent animal, but what are you trying to say Austin?

"Well, Clint that is the question? Sometimes we are the fully loaded double-barrel shotgun and sometimes we are the target. In this case, the past will decide which one of those becomes the narrative."

You got issues Austin, but I like it.

"Funny Clint, now you are starting to sound like IW. Haha!"

Yeah, he always told me I had issues, but that's why I was friends with him. Haaa!

"I know Clint, like you said, sometimes it just feels good to punch someone in the face with cold hard facts. Anyway, I was wondering if you heard more about any details of this Time travel trip or should I say Time Break expedition. I was interested in knowing what steps are involved for this time travel mission to possibly work."

Right, well here is the short version in understandable Scientific language that will spell out this risky, unstable, never been done before mission into the abyss. First, I needed to prepare warriors for this mission, which I have done for the most part. Second, a launch date has been established, which will happen in two days. Third, on the day of the launch, my Burendo Shotokan Warriors and I will step onto an oval-shaped iron cylinder of sorts. According to Gordon Scott, this cylinder has magnetic elements to it, which will aid in the process of leaving the earth. This means magnets have North and South Pole, so the opposite poles are attracted to each other, and the same poles repel each other. Simply put, we will have the same magnetic pole as the iron cylinder we are standing on. This is created by a clear liquid substance that has the same magnetic pole that will surround our bodies and will be ingested into our bodies' system. I guess in a weird Sci-Fi way we will be turned into a human magnet, but our bodies will be protected in this liquid pod that will give each of us life support to survive, and not age mentally or physically. Gordon Scott and other scientists and doctors were able to improve on this by studying me and the fact that I'm 113 years old but look pretty damn good.

Anyways, after this process is complete, the magnetic field will build, meaning the system will recognize that the iron cylinder and us(human) as the same magnetic pole. This occurs, as our bodies are encapsulated in the liquid magnetic substance that will repel the iron magnetic cylinder. This will begin the launch from the earth, and by the speed of light, we will in magician style disappear from the earth, and time travel to the selected wormhole in space. According to Scientists, we will be traveling 671 million miles per hour, but no G-force will occur. Anyways, even if there was G-force or other possible physical conditions, our bodies will be safe inside the time travel liquid pod. This includes exiting the earth in the year 2026 and reentry in the year 2086, so we don't just burn up or evaporate into nothing. At least that is what they are saying to us, although I'm not sold on that bullshit sandwich, and why would I be. As I was saying, we basically disappear from earth and are launched, this part I don't fully understand, but the course is programmed in by the use of geometry and mathematics to send us to the wormhole in space.

We will circle the rim of the wormhole, which is the gate way in different points in time space. During this time, the life pod will start to circulate, backward on the outer rim of the wormhole, generating enough force to avoid being sucked in. When the time travel liquid pod reaches a past time of 2026, we will be sucked into the wormhole, hopefully making it to the other side, and return to earth in the year 2026. As we are being sucked in, our magnetic pole switches to the opposite magnetic pole as the wormhole. You see, it has been discovered that space-time wormholes have a magnetic pole, so once we are locked into the year 2026, our magnetic pole will lock in, and only come out the other side of the wormhole in the year 2026. We will be pulled to Earth in the year 2026, which has a geomagnetic field around it. The north magnetic pole is into earth, so we will become the south magnetic pole or at least the magnetic liquid will do the trick. Opposites attract, there is a ton of scientific kung-fu involved and I might not be explaining it correctly, but either way, it sounds like a one-way ticket to Earth in the year 2026 or not. I guess my team and I will find out very soon.

"Wow! You and your warriors are brave souls to say the least, but that sounds like a mongoose entering a cobra's lair. Most of the time a mongoose goes into the cobra's nest, it never comes out. On a positive note, good luck."

You crack me up Austin, but the truth is the truth. Also, you would not know about this animated cartoon from 1975 called Rikki-Tikki-Tavi, which was about a mongoose, who has to enter a cobra's liar to save his family. Also, there were many short stories about this mongoose, who attempted a brave, stupid and dangerous thing, but we are doing just about the same thing. Entering the Alien(s) lair and risking everything to save everything and hopefully everyone.

"Quarantine breach! Quarantine breach! Zone 3! Evacuate to a safe area immediately!!!"

Ok Austin, another alarm breach, time to test out my Burendo Warriors again. Can't beat reality training. Assemble Burendo Shotokan Warriors, kill shot time is back in season! Time to clean the Fucking Dojo!!!

Austin, time for you to get to a safe location, my warriors and I have some kill shots to complete!

"I understand Clint, a man must know his limitations, and in my case, I will get to a safe area and let the pros do their Alien Zombie ass kicking!"

Exactly Austin!

Burendo Warriors be cautious in your approach, because this is the first time these Dead Adrenaline savages have breached a point in our security fence this far into our boundaries.

Ok, let's take a look at the savage subjects that just managed to get through the fenced-in area. Strange, looks to be only a few DAs on the other side of the border wall. I only see five of these alien abnormalities. Although outside the barriers, it looks to be at least 200-300 just waiting like hungry Were-coyotes. What the shit- sandwich is going on with these vessels of death. The ones standing outside the walls look to be in a catatonic state, but the five DA(s) that crashed our party are still actively ready for battle. Something isn't right. Burendo Warriors hold up and keep your position. These DA(s) seemed to want us to come to them. Nope, not today or any day. It is most definitely a trap to enjoy some prime-cut humans. Very odd indeed, never really noticed this before, but the red-eyed front-line DA workers look like they have a set of two right eyes in their head. Must have always been that way, but never really noticed it before. I guess some of these Dead Adrenaline Zombies just get that look in their eyes after the alien takes control of their mind and body.

You got to be kidding me, the female DA is speaking, and her eyes are morbid purple. Well, let's hear what she has to say. What unholy flashbacks do I hear coming from the female DA? I think my ears might be playing games. Her voice brings back memories of hearing Kris talking when she was all Hive Queened up. Holy shit!!! It is the Hive Queen all hosted up in a new human female body. Different body, but still that same creepy smile and sinister matter-of-fact cadence in her voice. Here we go, time to listen to the Bullshit song she is singing.

"Hello Clint, yes, it is me, your friendly neighborhood Hive Queen. I do love the title name you gave me, so I will take it, just like our alien race will take, dominate and transform this planet into ours. Yesss! What was the name given to you? Of course, "The Man Called Clint". Guess what Clint, our species are here to stay, and you will not survive the night. I will take your soul and the God you talk about you will never see it again. Time is up, and you will be breathing your last breath of life, along with every single weak insignificant Human, on the soon-to-be-altered face of planet Earth."

Yep, Hive Queen is back! Different body, but the same evil animal alien as before. Some things never change, even after 60 years or 60 minutes for that matter.

Oh well, things just got real in the year 2086, and a rare fuck steak sandwich is being served. Not really sure at this moment, but no time for uncertainties, only absolutes. Okay, time to reshuffle the deck, buy some time, and exit stage left.

Okay, Hive Queen for old time's sake will you answer a couple of questions. Come on, do it for Kris at the very least.

"I have to say, Clint, you are one interesting human, what a drive to control the conversation, and the outcome of your survival. It is so very amusing to see you struggle for answers, and possibilities for the human race to survive. Also, I still have Kris's memories and thought patterns intertwined with me forever. She did respect your will to survive, and did find you very entertaining at times, as I do. For this reason, as you would say "Don't Be a Dillweed" and ask your questions, but don't waste my time. Make no mistake, I thirst for the full drink from the chalice of total decimation of the human species, so make it quick!"

Ok, Hive Queeny, why is it that you are slowing down the process of taking human hosts? This means your front-line DA(s) are more violent in some ways, but they pick and choose who they will infiltrate and control. Almost as if they are waiting like controlled dogs.

"Now you are asking the right questions Clint. This gives me complete pleasure to answer. You see, death for the human race is a release from the suffering a human body endures during feeding time. You know what happened back in the year 2026. The bloodlust and the rapture that took place against your species were unquenchable You see, my solid red-eyed and bluish/red-eyed brothers and sisters couldn't quench their savage thirst for the human species. Meaning they cannot satisfy their urge, and appetite for human flesh, blood and bone."

"This was a miscalculation on our part. You see, this time my front-line workers are taking a more patient approach before attacking and consuming any humans. They will look for strong-minded people and only eat them if it is a last resort. The very weak humans are the first on the food table. The strong fortitude of humans will be eventually taken over to be a host. This is the thinning of the herd or groups in this case. In the year 2026, too many strong-minded or solid host humans were devoured. This left too many weak human hosts. This miscalculation had a most powerful outcome that left an army of DA organisms with an uncontrollable hunger for human flesh. You see when I had my front-line DA(s) gather at the Cracker plant or Hell's Gate as you called it Clint. I devoted much time to keeping my army controlled and focused.

This will not happen in the year 2086. You see, Clint, our race of supreme beings evolves and learns from our past deeds and failures. Unlike the disposable human race, which has retrogressed, and is rotting within, they are so very laughable and wasteful. Don't worry, Clint, my supreme alien race will stop this revolting calcification of the fragile human race. Hear me, Clint, so you feel the crippling pain that will be traveling your way. My front-line workers will only take the human hosts that are of solid minds and bodies."

"This will make for the best humans for our breeding purposes to continue the evolution of our species. The weak leftover humans will be dined on, and our celebration and world domination will be unstoppable. One more point of knowledge I possess, I know you and your Burendo Shotokan Warriors are attempting to time-travel back to the year 2026. I will be waiting with delight and anticipation for your arrival. Please survive the Time Break Expedition and find me. This is so very amusing to our species. You see, I know every move and technique you might attempt. Just by gathering more memories from the human host that I take over and control. In this case, I decided to take control of a lady who read your so-called journal for existence. You know who she is. Come on Clint. Take a good look at my host shell!"

Oh shit! You are one evil bag of hate and manipulation. You took over Liz Granites' body and mind just for information about our mission.

Liz Granite / AKA: Hive Queen 2086

"She wasn't as easy to take over as one would think based on her quiet outer personality, but internally Liz is a fighter, Clint."

Damn right Liz was a fighter, Hive bitch I will tell you this, you may sabotage a human being's mind and body, but you don't know everything. Meaning! It's time to clean the Fucking Dojo!!!! That's it! Burendo Shotokan Warriors. Time to eliminate these DA(s) and Hive Queen. Also, one more thing, Hive Queen 2086 is mine!

Looks like these DA(s) with Hive Queen are waiting for her to give the command to move in and battle. Wow, a lot more organized this time around than before. Back in the year 2026 these DA(s) would be trying to close the distance, so they could get the first bite of flesh off of a human femur bone. Not this time, they are more methodical in their attacks. Planning out each move and taking orders directly and consistently from their leader. Hive Queen is correct about how their alien species learned from past mistakes and have improved on the battle plan to annihilate the human race.

Burendo Warriors stay focused, put your fear in a compartment in your brain and leave it there locked away. These DA(s) are trying to enter your mind and break your will to survive. If that happens, then you will become one of those Zombie Alien shit sandwiches, which is worse than dying on the food table. Stay ready, stay strong, maintain unshakable fortitude to survive this day.

   Pick out your DA of choice, and end this destructive force of hate, sadness and suffering. Leave none of them standing, let's send a message to Hive Queen that we have looked for the signs, and have the ability to adapt, and improve from our past mistakes too. May your strikes be fluent and unflinching this day we battle. Let's do this, Time to Clean the Fucking battle ground Dojo!!!

   Let's see how my Burendo Shotokan Warriors do this day in real combat, in the Dead Adrenaline zone. I believe their skills are honed and ready for the challenge. They need to be on their fight game and never give in to the terror that awaits.

Miscalculation On A Massive Level

Year 2086

Ok, it's kill shot time. Wow, Silas just took out one of the DA bodyguards with Hive bitch. Gavenitely gave this DA a nice low-spinning wheel kick (Gedan Ushiro Uranium Mawashi Geri) to the outer calf then a second kick. This time landing a high spinning Wheel kick (Chudon Ushiro Ura Mawashi Geri) to the neck area of this DA. Unlike some other similar kicks of this nature the leg is mostly straight and extended out like a completed side kick, except the foot isn't arched and the ankle is straight. Using a fantastic wheel kick motion, hitting with the heel of the foot. Followed by a 6-strike combination of closed-knuckled hammer fist strikes (Tettsui) with knife hand strikes (Shuto-Uchi) sprinkled in. Working without hesitation to find the kill spot and then it happened. A nice Tiger Paw (Tora No Te Uchi) whack to the right ear area of the DA. The last sound this "Dill Weed DA" heard was death. All topped off with Silas giving this DA his last rights, ending with a blessing. Silas is definitely ready for the mission.

Let's see, where did the Hive Queen disappear to? Really, more catch me if you can bullshit. Hive Queen is playing mind games with a twist of avoidance again. A disturbing outcome, but I am not going to take the bait. She wants me to track her down and distract me from my mission. Nope, not in the year 2086. I will pick up her trail in the year 2026 and end this creepy death match for good.

Looks like my other Burendo Warriors are working great as a team. Two more DA(s) just got destroyed. Sandra, Logan and Oliver decided to each take a turn with unstoppable kicking prowess. They utilized the three first

47

kicks any solid martial artist should know. Front kick (Mae-Geri), side kick (Yoko-Geri) and roundhouse kick (Mawashi- Geri). Launching each kick with high, middle and low placement. Jodon (High), Chudon (Middle) and Gedan (Low). They land these kicks with absolute target placement and without mercy. There it is, Sandra zoned in on the kill shot area quickly with a high sidekick (Jodon Yoko-geri), dropping down on her rear hand and kicking upward underneath the neck/chin area. Hapkido style of kicking, where the foot is up high, and the body is down out of sight. Lights out! Then Sandra, decided on spinning Ushiro-ri (back kick) to the back of the upper rib cage area of the last DA dipshit, causing the DA to collapse forward, but not completely shut down. Within seconds, Oliver drove a high knee shot to the same back rib area.

Upon impact, Logan went for the kill and ended it with a downward ridge hand separating the ribs and crushing the soft spot on this dragon DA. Have to say, Sandra has a Sixth Sense when it comes to finding the kill spot. Although it did take a lot more hits to destroy these DAs, these creatures from another planet must be adapting and becoming harder to kill. Speaking of Sixth Sense, this reminds me of the 1999 physiological thriller *Sixth Sense,* starring one of the most powerful actors *Bruce Willis.* Directed by M. Night Shyamalan, who is known for twisted surprise endings. Anyway, I definitely see dead people, but they have major adrenaline issues. Plus, this human condition we are living in, unfortunately will have a surprise ending that will shake our souls to the edge of extinction if we don't keep the faith, and kick-ass.

Ok, there's Olivia and Sullivan heading towards the other DA waiting to pounce. Nice, Olivia just completed a perfect Yoko-Tubi Geri (Flying/jumping sidekick) to the head this DA. Knocking him down onto the ground, and just like that Sullivan finished the job by placing Shitamuki-no-ashibumi (Downward foot stomps) from the top of the DA head, down to his waistline. Just so happens the foot stomp placed to the left of the solar plexus did the kill-shot deed, and the lights are shut off.

Great work Burendo Shotokan Warriors. The technique is looking top notch, and the teamwork meshes well. Ok, it's time to get to the command room and get briefed on our options before launch time. Based on what just occurred. We need to haul ass out of the year 2086 and get to the year 2026, because as you all heard, Hive Queen will be waiting, so we need to surprise attack the shit sandwich aliens and start this journey sooner. Although maybe this is what the Hive Queen wants us to do. Damn future affects the past and the past affects the future. Reminds me of the 2005 movie, *A Sound of Thunder,* starring Catherine *McCorma,* Ben Kingsley, and Edward Burns. This movie's premise was that micro actions can lead to mammoth consequences, which is so true. Time travel is no joke, so we all must be very careful not to break anything in the year 2026, except for the Hive Queen's face! Burendo Shotokan Warriors see you at the command room in 20 minutes. Get your gear and be ready. We are leaving with or without approval.

Ok, I just made it back to the command room and I am ready to rock and roll off this future stage. Elvis Presley definitely rocked and rolled off a past stage. It's time to make future history in the past if that makes any kind of sense. Perfect, there is Austin.

Hey Austin, the team is leaving now. The Hive Queen is here, and she knows our plans to stop her in the past.

49

How do I know this to be true, because I just spoke with the Hive Bitch, and she has taken over Liz Granite as a host. As you know, Liz has been involved in every step of this mission planning, so it can be documented and recorded with complete accuracy. Liz's expertise in this area made her a walking Wikipedia, so Hive Queen has every detail. Not good, but my Burendo Warriors and I need to go because Hive Queen is waiting here right in the future. Our only chance to battle this alien sicko is in the past. Get Gordon Scott here, and all of the non-time traveling Time Break Expedition people on this project here. This bullshit sandwich is a mess, and we need to make a move now!

"Holy Excalibur Shit Sandwich indeed Clint. The gathering notification has been sent. They are on their way and will be here sooner than a mosquito's ass hitting an open palm strike (Teisho- Uchi). How do you like my Japanese Clint?" I get it, Austin, it keeps you going. Now shut up and let's make this happen.

"Yessiree!"

What's the holdup Austin and where are your mission launch people?

"Here they come now Clint."

That's an average response time, but my Burendo Warriors, Cool Blue and I are ready to go, so let's get his time travel shit party started.

Great, here we go. Looks like a High-ranking Commander and his low-level military thugs are coming my way. Not in the mood for red tape backward stupidity.

"Mmm, so you are the Man called Clint. Not impressed, you see I am Commander Stenson Samuel Sigourney

50

Weaver. I'm the top military leader in charge of this mission launch. Nothing happens, unless I give the command."

Wow! That is some funny ass shit. Is it me or do people of the future have long ass names and titles. Although "The Man Called Clint" is a pretty long title name that is definitely bad ass.

Ok, Commander Dill-Weed. Two things, first, the only thing cool about you is the Sigourney Weaver part of your long-ass name, which is most definitely one of the best badass actresses of my time. Sigourney Weaver was in hit movies like the 1979 Alien and 1992 Aliens. She acted in many other top-shelf movies and my opinion one of the first female lead badasses to ever Ur-raken-uchi (backfist) the big screen. I bet she would think that Hive Queen was "*a bitch*." The second thing, I don't give a shit-sandwich about your position to launch now or not to launch. I don't have the time, and really don't care; the past is waiting for the future to arrive. Wow, I do reference Sigourney Weaver a lot in my talked-out thoughts. Might even be repetitive. Oh well, keeps me going.

What's wrong? Did I confuse you with my movie trivia and Japanese terminology? Guess not, because things just got real again. Commander Knuckle Nuts just went into a catatonic state. His eyes are changing back and forth as Mr. Breakfast Man did back in the year 2026. No fire pit, and no breakfast this time, but the same state of animation. Just like I thought, Commander Stenson Samuel was weak-willed and checked out. I left Sigourney Weaver out of his full name because there's nothing weak-willed about her. Looks like his military men and women with him are also in the beginning stages of the alien possession.

Time to move, ok there's Gordon Scott. Gordon, we need to launch now. There's no time to explain, but Hive Queen is here, so Burendo Warriors and I are in position for launch as practiced. You need to send us back to the year of 2026 Beaver County, PA. Make sure to lock in a time that was before the major onset of the alien infection,

"You got it Clint; the launch code has been sent. In 60 seconds, you will be encapsulated in a travel pod and launched into the past. The target bullseye will be the wormhole to the past. Sounds simple, but it's not. Hope it works, but if it doesn't, we are all doomed. Also, Clint, no matter what happens you must not encounter yourself in the past. This could be devastating in an unknown way. "

"You see, none of the Burendo Shotokan Warriors existed in the year 2026, but your past self does. For this reason, avoid your past self at all costs to humankind. No matter how careful you and your team are, arriving in the past will cause the future to shift, but the least amount of time travel damage caused, will only hopefully slightly change the future. On the other side of the earth's coin, your mission is to stop the Hive Queen for good, so the future doesn't include her, and her alien trolls.

We don't know the future outcome if Hive Queen is eliminated permanently, but we do know the outcome if she survives. Our choices are one chance or no chance. The one chance of survival is unknown, but no chance is occurring now."

Thanks, Gordon, I get it, Time to unleash the Kraken, but make sure he wears quiet shoes. Let's get the DA party started.

Shit' my poor friend Austin looks to be changing into a savage beast and is now going after Gordon. Fuck no! The command area is getting smashed and destroyed all around them. Also, Commander knuckle nuts and his military people have changed, and are flipping the fuck salad out. I know I said fuck salad instead of fuck sandwich, I guess I'm trying to speak healthier. Sorry, humor keeps me going. Ok, the area where the launch code was sent looks to have been damaged. The final countdown has begun. Great song by the way. 1986 release, Album (The Final Countdown), by the Swedish rock band Europe. The song was featured in the 1985 movie Rocky IV (4), (Shi). Enough song and movie nostalgia for now. Ok, time to get back to the Final*******Countdown! Too late now, no return my body is trapped in the time travel pod magnetic liquid. Here goes everything.

   I will survive the night, til the morning lite.

"5(Go), 4(Shi), 3(San) ,2(Ni), 1(Ichi)————————Launching completed, Time Break Expedition is a go. System failure, System failure! Separated Geographic Coordinates system malfunction! ——————————————————————
System shutting down in three seconds.
3(San),2(Ni),1(Ichi)————offline pending reboot."

The Return Of Pain and Suffering

Year 2026

"The smell of burnt plastic and metal floats in a large oval cloud from the ground upwards. As it slowly dissipates a human body appears dressed in a futuristic combat-style uniform, lying face down in a wooded area. Circling this human form is a crop circle shape, leafless trees are scattered throughout the woods standing high, but are dead and rotting. Slowly the human body in the woods starts to move and shake in a violent, but systematic fashion. Suddenly Logan's eyes open, and he stops shaking and sits up. This confused human being stands up and starts to walk towards an open grass area, which leads to a roadway, where a vehicle is parked on the roadside. This human walks over to the parked car and sees an individual slumped over behind the steering wheel. The passenger side door is opened by the curious confused human dressed in field combat attire. He enters the vehicle to check for life signs, then it happens without warning! The unconscious human inside the parked vehicle awakens and opens his eyes. Blood is oozing from the vessels inside his solid red eyes, and feeding time has arrived, human steak is on the menu. The battle for survival of the human race begins and hand strikes are deployed by the uniformed human, who is attempting to land a kill shot. The savage infected human loves the taste of human flesh, and is unstoppable, as each bite and tear of its mouth viciously celebrates its victory. Quickly and accurately, this crazed infected human punctures through the combat uniform. Then with the swiftness of a panther and strength of a grizzly bear, the last bite is applied. The neck area is locked onto, and blood begins to fill the front area of the vehicle, covering the floorboards like a spigot spraying violently and without mercy. Suddenly the human

54

dressed in combat uniform is flung back and forth inside the vehicle like a fragile human made of glass. With one last powerful movement, the red-eyed human shatters the front windshield with the broken body of the lifeless human and pounces onto the front hood of the vehicle. The neck is still being bitten by the cannibalistic human. The lifeless human is dragged off into the woods and slammed into a tree. Then the red-eyed savage continues to feed, eat, and devour as much as consumption would allow. Then with a creepy and clever movement, this Zombified human awkwardly climbs up a tree next to the poor deceased human body as if to wait for its next victim. Within the bloody scraps of what is left of the human carcass, an embroidered human body symbol is covered slowly by blood draining from the dead human's body. This human dressed for battle learned a life-ending lesson. The anatomy of the human body is weak and pathetic against a foreign organism."

Enough Said About That

Year 2026

What fuck the sandwich just happened, my eyes are burning slightly, and my mind is racing. Ok, got it. We are here in the year 2026, just trying to wake up from the time travel wormhole experience. Not really that cool, felt like I was underwater, and my ears popped. Then within seconds, the space ride was over, the worst part was the evacuation of that magnetic liquid substance that projectiles out of your mouth like a waterfall. At least, it leaves the human body's system quickly. There he is my boy Cool Blue going around and waking up my warrior team. mm, yes speaking of time travel this reminds me of the 1960 movie *The Time Machine,* except in that movie the main character traveled forward into the future. Been there and done that. Funny, I have traveled back in time to the year 2026, but I originally came from this year or time, based on this I still haven't traveled back to a year I have never been before. Ok getting a little into time travel weeds, which can confuse the hell out of someone. Let's see how the Burendo Shotokan Warriors are doing. Yep, time for a nickname. I'm going to call my elite fighters. SW(s) Sensei's Warriors. Ok, Blue, give me a status check for the lifelines of each SW.

Shit, it looks like we are missing two from our team, Silas and Logan. On a more solid note, according to Cool Blues data, we are just outside of Beaver County PA, in the year 2026. Ok, SW(s) get your mind and body collected and gather around me. Apparently, just before we launched the code got mixed up, due to the computer program and equipment getting damaged as many of you witnessed back in the year 2086. Silas and Logan were separated

56

during entry into the year 2026. They did manage to land in Beaver County PA. in the year 2026 but were taken out and are now deceased. Each of you is equipped with the optic lens in your dominant eye, so you can see visually and hear some audio of what Blue sees. Blue is recording events as they play out, so a record of these events is documented. That being said, Cool Blue can see and retrieve visual and audio as it is occurring or after it has transpired. Meaning Blue can see and hear what you individually are witnessing, because of this, Blue is going to play back in each of your assigned optic lenses the footage of what Silas and Logan were visualizing as they were dying. Graphic in nature, but this needs to be watched, so you know what we're up against.

(Total silence feels the air as each of the Burendo Shotokan Warriors see and hear the footage of how Silas death. Then the team watched the footage of Logan's death, as it unfolded before them.)

  Ok, now all of you know this enemy we are about to battle takes many forms and will not hesitate to remove your flesh from your bones. If you manage to avoid skinning, then your mind and body may be taken as a host, which is the worst fate in my opinion. The third option of death is getting bit and dying slower by way of poisoning your blood, which isn't pleasant either, as you all witnessed in the year 2086. What does this mean? It means for all of you to get your head totally out of your assessment and focus with complete mind and body.

  You must, without interruption and fear, keep your will and strength to survive. Remember this Burendo Shotokan Warriors and never forget!!!!

  Ok, enough said about that, now account for your gear, get fueled with food and drink, then it will be time to move. Based on the video footage, it is without a doubt, Silas that got eaten alive by a gang of fucked up birds, and all that was left was the Gold embroidered cross symbol from his warrior uniform. In reference to Logan's death, everyone observed his mangled body and remains within the bloody mess left. Logan's embroidered Human body symbol indicates further evidence of his death. Now on another important point, we are at the beginning of the first day of the human infection I witnessed back in 2026, the first time I experienced it.

In fact, I killed that DA that dismembered, and consumed Logan. That was the disabled vehicle, dead body, and DA I dealt with 60 years ago or 60 minutes ago. Give or take days or weeks in between, before arriving in the year 2086. Meaning, I was in the year 2026, my first go around, and found the body by the tree. Wild to think that the person lying dead by the tree was Logan. Damn, crazy time travel shit, really can get in a person's head.

Both Silas and Logan were good men and knew the risk, but now I believe they are in **GOD's** hands, and I hope they are enjoying the fresh air in heaven. You see, just like the memory of Silas's embroidered Golden Cross and Logan's embroidered Human body symbol that they wore with honor and fortitude. Don't forget them, and the knowledge they brought to this mission. Ok, Burendo Shotokan Warriors, say your goodbyes emotionally, and we need to keep moving on this mission.

On a lighter note, not to change the subject too much, I know one thing a big cup of coffee from the Coffee *Beanery* located in Center Township would give me the kick I need. This would bring me back to life. Definitely a great tasting brew, and fantastic owner and staff. Best in Beaver County PA.

Coffee Beanery

Sorry, SW(s) about past thoughts blended with caffeine, it keeps me going. Before we head out. Do any of you have any questions?

"I do Sensei Clint."

Yes, what do you got Olivia?

"Not a question, but a valuable set of information that each one needs to know before we embark on this mission. While Sensei was talking to all of us, I ran a complete, and thorough lifespan check on each of us including myself. The findings were distressing and bizarre, to say the least. If my health calculations are correct, all of us except Sensei Clint are starting to reverse in age. Our bodies will become younger as each day passes. Meaning this process will happen at an extreme rate. What I'm trying to say in a kind and gentle manner is that by day four of this mission. We will have reversed age by 30 years. As we all know, none of us are over the age of 29. Meaning in four days, we will no longer exist. How that takes place is unknown, and what happens to our bodies is even more puzzling. I'm going to keep running data on each of our life spans to see if there's a way to stop or at least slow the process down.

In reference to Sensei not being affected, it might have something to do with him coming back to a year where he does exist already or the fact that he traveled back to this year of 2026 already being of the age of 113 when we left. Either way, he is only aging at a normal rate forward. I know my friends; this is one tough painful pill to swallow. So very sorry for this news."

Holy medieval sandwich didn't see that one coming Olivia. Top notch work and keep trying to find a possible answer. My thought on why I didn't get affected by this type of reverse age illness was because of something Hive Queen did to me when I was placed in that catatonic state and preserved for 60 years. We don't know for sure, but I do know one thing within this conversation we are having. In the next couple of days, I will be running a daycare center, and by day four you poor souls will cease to exist. We need to move and speed up this ass-kicking of these aliens. Time isn't on our side, especially for you guys.

"This is, screwed up man! I'm not on board with any of this. First Silas and Logan meet at the Grim Reapers hotel. They checked in, but never will check out. What the Fuck, we need to focus on trying to find a way to get back to the year of 2086."

Cool your emotional jets, Oliver!

You are the Mathematician that knows more about the Time Break Expedition than any of us. I might be the leader of this SW unit, but you have the handle on some of the possibilities of returning, even though they have said it is a one-way time travel mission. Also, maybe some of that mathematical bullshit could be helpful to Olivia when trying to figure out the reverse age shit-fest coming your way. I would say to stop acting like a man-baby, but it might be too soon for baby jokes, if you know what I mean.

"Well Sensei Clint, that's a hard line, but you're right, so I will put my mind into helping the cause. I will say this though, there is a possible way to return to the year 2086. In each of our remaining gear bags is a Time-traveling liquid-forming pod. Also, a collapsible magnetic metal plate is with the pod. The metal plate is very lightweight, and collapses down to the size of a quarter, but will expand to the needed size. Meaning if activated, it will form around our bodies and the magnetic field will be obtained, just like it did on our departure time travel flight from the year 2086. In this case, we would be leaving the year 2026, and going to the future. When this occurs, the speed of light signal will be sent back to the year 2086, directly to the command center of the launch. Hopefully, the system does reboot and is still functioning. The code for a return launch will be activated, and we make it back.

I don't know with absolute certainty if this would even work, but it is a possibility. Gordon Scott placed these return time travel pods in each of our gear bags, he told me not to reveal this information, unless it was our only option. You see, he didn't want to cloud our judgments on this mission. According to Gordon, this type of time travel return technology to go forward into the future was untested, and in its infant stages. However, some of the technology behind Cool Blue was incorporated, so the alien organisms couldn't shut down the power source for the time travel pod or at least slow down their attempts.

Sorry, I lost my mindset for a moment, and that was pretty funny dropping a baby joke Sensei, given we are a couple days from being back in diapers. Also, the possibility of time travel pods that take us back to the future are still in the "infant" stages. *Infant*, yep, I just said that one, Fucked up, but funny."

Yea, now you're cooking with free will fuel Oliver and cracking some jokes. Good to know some positive possibilities for the SW crew. Listen people if I'm still kicking, and you guys and girls become too young to understand. I will personally launch your time travel pod and give you a second chance in life. Even though you might not like what you find in the year 2086, for now let's stay on course, and get this mission completed. Speaking of going back to the future.

It reminds me of the American 1985 Science Fiction film, *Back to the Future,* starring Michael J. Fox. In this movie, they time-traveled from the year 1985 to 1955 but eventually needed to go back to the future year of 1985. Kinda like what's happening now, except we traveled from the year 2086 to the year 2026, and for better or worse, you my Burendo Shotokan Warriors might have to be sent back to the future year of 2086 if baby land shows up. I have already left the year 2026 by way of alien time travel and ended up in the year 2086. I have now returned to the year 2026 to complete this mission and have no plans of leaving until this alien bullshit takeover is stopped. Also, if you think about if I would stay here, there would be two of me permanently. Crazy, I never really thought out what I would do if this mission were a success. I guess I will figure that out when I cross that mental-thought bridge. On the other hand, maybe I will have to fight myself to the death, but if I win the fight, and take myself out. I guess I won't exist anymore. See humor works, remember that Burendo Shotokan Warriors. Ok, any other questions, before we embark on this mission?

Sullivan, you have anything you want to say or add that is useful.

"No, I'm good, I will run some data tests to see if any method or science behind this reverse age issue can show a pattern that could be broken. Like I said, Sensei Clint I'm good and ready to stomp down some of these aliens."

Sandra, how about you? You have been very quiet like a cougar lining up its sight line to destroy its prey.

"I was Sensei, since we landed back in time, I have been running a check scan on the terrain we must cover, and the possible location of the Hive Queen entity, and her first host, I believe you called him Alien Boss Man and it was the first time you witnessed the purple eye strangeness."

This is why I picked you for this mission Sandra, always thinking forward, and setting up for the next move. So, what did you come up with Sandra in reference to our present location?

"Ok, we ended up smack dab in an open field surrounded by woods, or should we say the Pennsylvania forest. If my calculations and coordinates are correct, this large open area is somewhere in a place called Zelienople, PA," which is approximately 35 miles, via Route 68. The Time travel pods must be designed to find an open field or forest area to drop off the human cargo, strange thing Sensei, in the areas where each of us landed a large circular pattern has formed around that area."

No shit, I wouldn't believe it if I didn't see it for myself. Those circular formation aren't just any type of shape. They are what we used to call crop circles back in my time, and if memory serves me, there are tons of studies done that indicated a magnetic field was present in the area of the crop circles. They popped up all over the United States, and other places in the world. Some thought they were man-made, and some thought it was from an alien race. Now I know it was from the "Cow Machine Project" that Gordon Scott talked about. Testing out the time travel pods caused a lot of cows to be mangled up, but when they started to survive. Those crop circles were left behind. Funny, the crop circles were created by humans, but did come from the future. Wrap your brain around that one.

On a more nostalgic thought, the town of Zelienople brings back some great memories. Such great storefronts on the Main Street, hell Zelienople is in western Butler County, but oh so close to western Beaver County. Luckily, they are just outside the terminal realm, but it looks like a ghost town. I bet the USCM (United States Controlled Military) evacuated them just for safety precautions. Plus, as we all know, the entire State of Pennsylvania becomes part of the terminal realm eventually, whether it was infected or not.

There it is, the Main Street of Zelienople, it looks to be silent, but in perfect working order. Let's see, there is the Little Green bookstore. Fantastic place to get a book to capture your imagination in any genre. The owner definitely knows books and gives a person a great opportunity to read their favorites. Also, the Little Green bookstore is Author-friendly and supports and helps new and upcoming Authors. Mmm? I wonder if they have a copy of Dead Adrenaline: One Man's Journey To Survive Beaver County, PA. Now that would be a great book to read, especially during the Dead Adrenaline apocalypse. This book definitely needs to be written.

The Little Green Bookstore

Best Seller

Yep, I am getting lost in the story telling again, I better put my thoughts of books back on the bookshelf. Time to put my focus towards the punishing consequences awaiting my team, and I in the terminal realm of Beaver County, PA.

Ok, at least we dropped in from the future in a nice quiet out-of-the-way area. Less chance of being discovered. It's probably a stone's throw from Route 68. Sandra, see how far from Route 68 we are and the quickest way to get to it. I know exactly where we are at but plot a course to Beaver County. Find a section of the fence/barricade that is less guarded by the United States Controlled Military (USCM). We are close to Zelienople airport I believe, but flying would be a very bad idea given the last plane I saw crashed into the Vanport Bridge in Beaver County. PA.

"Yes Sir, I will plot a course to RT. 68 and also find some transportation along the way."

Ok Sandra.

Warriors, we are minus two of our team. Sad, but this is the world we are living in, so prepare your mind and body for more casualties. Never give up or hesitate, because these alien assholes are waiting in the blood shadows for our souls.

Cool Blue, fly ahead and check out the area for a possible vehicle, and send this information back to Sandra. She will plot a course to that location. Use your chameleon color changes and blend in with the terrain. I don't want to alarm anyone that is trying to survive in the terminal realm.

Definitely cool upgrades done to Blue, IW would love this. Now Cool Blue find some Steel and Wheels if possible.

"Sensei! I just got data back from Cool Blue, it looks like he located an area along the border fence into the terminal realm (AKA: Beaver County, PA) that isn't protected as much, and appears to be away from large groups of USCM soldiers. Looks to only have three soldiers in the area."

67

Wow, Cool Blue works fast. Ok, Sandra, this sounds like our entry point into the terminal realm. Burendo Shotokan Warriors let's move and be prepared for things to travel into the domain of unpredictable consequences. You see what we are about to do isn't for the weak souls, you must all remember what I have taught you, and no matter what happens the good of the team outweighs the good of the one. Meaning, if we stay strong and remain a Yosai (fortress) for good, evil will never stop this mission. Does everyone understand this and what I mean, because if you don't you will become a liability to our safety and success.

"Sensei, all of us understand, and are prepared to get this mission completed."

Thanks for the feedback, Olivia, and it's good to know everyone is on the same page. We will see if this continues as this mission of death unfolds.

Violence Has a Friend

Year 2026

Sensei's log, Throwing star-date 2026. My Sensei Warriors and I have time-traveled from the year 2086 back to the year 2026. The "Time Break Expedition" ion" wasn't a success upon entry into the atmosphere of death. Both team members Silas and Logan were separated from the rest of the unit. When this occurred, they met the savagery, and death from this upside-down world, no life signs were found upon a life scan done by Doctor Olivia, and technology from Cool Blue. Our mobile sick bay is empty for the time being. However, an unexpected age reversing illness has taken over the rest of the Burendo Shotokan Warriors. For some unexplained reason, I haven't been inflicted with this regression in age illness. We are day one into the beginning stages of the alien virus infection. In four days, the Hive Queen will continue her path to the year 2086, based on the battle that occurred with my past self at the One Strike Karate dojo. This timeline must be altered, and the Hive Queen must be stopped. Sensei log, signing off.

"Sensei Clint, we are standing on the outskirts of the barricades of the border into Beaver County in a wooded area just off of State Route 68. Looks like three USCM members are in the area with high powered weaponry. Based on intelligence, they have orders to kill anyone within a 1-mile radius of the border. Also, they will shoot to kill anyone attempting to enter the terminal realm, in fact, archive records indicate that back in the first go around in the year 2026, residents/humans of the year 2026, attempted to enter the terminal realm into Beaver County, PA, but were killed. Public opinion was mixed, but the overall thought was that entry into the terminal realm could spread this infection, so the family members and friends of

69

the people trapped in the Beaver County terminal realm were taken out if they attempted entry. Some backlash occurred, but the Government crushed any retaliation. Also, family members were paid out a large amount of currency to keep quiet."

Some things never change, and the wheels of shady government power keep rolling along. Good update Sandra. Now we know an entry point and unfortunate shoot-to-kill orders by the USCM. Time to take an armored military vehicle, and break through the entrance gate opening into the Terminal Realm. Cool Blue, fly past a couple of those soldiers standing by that armored Humvee. Distract the hell out of them and we will do the rest. SW's no kill shots, just knockout blows.i

Don't hurt the soldiers too badly, they are just following orders from the government elite. Although you would think free will would guide them to do the right thing. Oh shit! What terrible timing, it looks to be several citizens attempting to get through the gate. Must be trying to get to some of their family or friends quarantined in the terminal realm. They are about to get annihilated by way of target practice. Let's move SW's. If those soldiers start shooting civilians. Kill shots are back in season by way of Burendo Shotokan excellence. Shit! We are a little bit of a distance from those USCM soldiers, so if they start raining firepower onto the civilians. We won't close the distance in time to stop them.

Although Sandra, Sullivan and Olivier have covered some ground quickly, and are getting pretty close to the soldiers.

Not good, Olivia, take cover into the tree line, because those soldiers are starting to send rounds towards Sandra, Olivier and Sullivan, which could strike us in the distance. Looks like they are pinned down, luckily, they were able to judo roll behind that Armored Humvee and Cool Blue buzzed by them numerous times, which confused them for a moment. On the flip side of the death coin, the soldiers are closing the distance on them now.

Anyways, this distraction gave those civilians a chance to escape into the land of the terminal realm. Based on what's waiting for them, it might have been better if they had been shot. Sounds cruel and harsh, but DA Town is no joke.

Ok, Sullivan is contacting me in the short distance via optic eye communication. Its audio and video capabilities are Iris Warrior worthy.

"Sensei, Sullivan here, I only have a few seconds, the soldiers are moving in and we're getting ready to deploy our throwing stars and the "Han'i Ha" weapon of choice is ready to go, depending on how close we can get to take out these soldiers."

Sounds good Sullivan, aim for the neck area / throat area. Sandra and Oliver gain access to the Armored Humvee (AKA Steel & Wheels). If no keys are found, then one of those soldiers has them. Hot wire if you have too, Olivia and I will be running the tree line edge and will be at your back in a few seconds. Sensei out.

Ok, time for some long distant combat ax action. Going to double spin with a locked wrist and nail the soldier that looks to be in charge. Nice connection with his left inner thighs area. He will be sure to bleed out. Yes, fantastic throwing star connection to a second soldier's front throat area by Sullivan.

Ok two down, and it looks like one more soldier standing. Oh no! You got to be kidding! If I am correct, it looks like this soldier is armed with a L7A2 General Purpose Machine Gun (GPMG). This is the British Military weapon of choice. One deadly style Machine gun, I guess the USCM decided to use them too. Looks like he is going prone and has it almost set up for the kill. At least Sandra got the keys off one of the dead soldiers, but we need to go before our bodies turn to Swiss cheese. Also, I bet they have to radio in for backup. Ok SW's let's load up in the Steel and wheels and get the fuck salad/sandwich out of here. Yep, now I'm speaking healthy and unhealthy. Fuck it, you got to have a balance. Hell, who knows if a salad is healthier than a sandwich now's days. Time to Move!

"I got this Sensei, 4 seconds out from smashing this gate over."

Drive fast Olivier, because the GPMG rounds are here. I hear the rounds ringing off the metal-plated Steel and Wheels.

"Sensei! Our back left tire just got tagged, it's deflating as we speak."

I hear you, Olivia, Olivier keep moving, until the wheels fall off this steel wagon. We need to get outside the one-mile radius within the terminal realm, even though the soldiers' fire power might be shut down, due to alien interference. Distance will tell the tale.

"Engine problems Sir, those Machine gun rounds have damaged the inner workings of the Humvee. We are losing fluids, which causing us to slow down."

Ok, it looks like the Soldier ran partially into the terminal realm area. Looks to be getting ready to set up again for a prone fire Might have a jam in the Machine Gun because he has stopped firing. SW's stay in the Steel and Wheels, drive it as far as it will go. I will catch up with you in a few. I need to end this, if any more rounds are fired at the Humvee. Sylvania Hills Cemetery will be our new house, based on the rounds flying into the terminal realm, and hitting Humvee, the alien animals decided to let the firepower work within that one-mile radius for now. Also, if this soldier survives. He will know about us, and the Government dill-weeds will send in the reinforcements, which might stir the DA hive too much, and alter the future. Don't need the future-time boat rocked too much if possible. Now it makes sense.

Those soldiers weren't going to shoot those civilians entering the terminal realm. They didn't care if they made it through. Just another way for this whole Governmental cover-up to quiet the public. They figured those civilians would get taken out in the terminal realm, even if they attempted to make it back out. Target practice would commence. Fucked up, but why wouldn't it be, elections brew treacherous consequences. On the flip side, the USCM wants to stop us. Maybe because they know we are the "Alpha Dog" and might succeed in unlocking this cover up, and let the world know. Mmm? I have to revisit that thought at a later time. Might be a different approach to help prevent or at least make people aware of what is to come in the future, so they can prepare each generation to look for the signs, Ok time to kick ass on down the road,

"Hai Sensei, we will keep moving."

Great Sandra, you're in charge, keep moving, and find the location of Big Boss man. We need its location pin down, so our next move can be made. When he is located, the Hive Queen might have already taken his soul and invaded his mind and body. This would be the first stage of infiltration. The second stage will include two, large size purple/bloody-looking floating jellyfish sacks. As all of you know from our many hours of briefing you have got to be ready for this battleground if these jellyfish enter Big Boss Man's mind and body.

73

Hive Queen will be at full alien asshole power. Last bit of advice, remember to stay focused and be on high alert, DAs are around, and it is feeding time!

I will catch up with you guys and gals, but it is time to end this machine gun dill-weed!!

Well, it's just me again alone in the wasteland of the terminal realm. My SW(s) are out of sight, and no DA(s) are around yet, but they will be showing up. Crazy, I just must love to talk to myself out loud, maybe this is my post-traumatic stress, based on what I've been through, and witnessed. Who am I kidding, I haven't been a witness this whole time really, I have been a participant.

Hell Yea! I've been the cure against this disease. Plus, I talked to myself out loud, long before this shit storm of DA(s) came to town. This reminds me of the 1986 American film *Cobra*, starring Sylvester Stallone. In this movie, Crime was the disease and Cobra was the cure. Definitely what's been happening to humanity is a crime, so now it's time to find the cure. Ok, I got lost in the movie sauce again. Good thing, I talk fast because Dill-weed machine gunner is trying to get his weapon of choice unjammed, and then it is open season on "The Man Called Clint." I bet it's not a weapon jam, those alien entities know how to fuck up someone's plan.

Luckily their voodoo magic is helping me this time, or maybe that's what these alien dill-weeds want to happen. You never know when you're facing this level of evil. Time to move in for the kill.

What medieval mayhem is this before me? This soldier just went red-eyed on me. Meaning feeding time has arrived again in DA town. Oh shit! This DA soldier decided to go Rambo on me and picked up the GPMG machine gun from the ground. Now he is standing there with a

74

savage fangoria-looking face of suffering and happiness. A Deformed smirk is coming across his face. Man, his eyes are really blood-red with rage. Speaking of Rambo, the 1982 movie *First Blood* starring Sylvester Stallone playing the role of John Rambo has just floated into my mind. Crazy, I've never really seen a red-eyed DA use common sense and decide to be logical. Case in point, bring a GPMG (General Purpose Machine Gun) to a fight involving "The Man Called Clint." Pretty fucking logical in my opinion. OK, let's hope that the Machine gun hasn't been switched back on by the alien invader buddies.

Time to take cover, because this logical dumbass DA just shot some rounds into the sky. I guess target practice is back on in the terminal realm. Must be a learning curve for these aliens to use our weapons.

Although I'm sure it won't take long for the alien entity to tap into the soldier host.

Yep, here it comes, a DA soldier is letting loose with rounds now, and they are heading in my direction. Fuck, this is going to end badly. No really good place for solid cover. True, *Sometimes Zombies Don't Come From The Grave. Ok,* I got to kangaeru (think) fast, and with shuchu (focus) to survive (ikinokoru).

Now this DA is toying with me. He is shooting everywhere but at me. After each flurry of rounds being fired. A hideous scream of suffering and happiness is unleashed. Fuck this, throwing time, just landed it in the neck of the DA. Not a kill shot, but man is their blood squirting out everywhere. Now the DA is pissed off and aiming the Machine Gun at me. Just launched my combat ax at him. Landed it in his right arm. Looks to have taken the arm clean off, just below the elbow. Future Steel is very sharp and deadly, he must have been a right-handed shooter. Now it is time to move in and end this.

Got my Han'i Ha" deployed at 4 ft range and sword-slicing action will commence. Going to slice off his left arm. No arms with hands attached, means no trigger figure. Too bad, but I'm not sad. That is just the way it is in DA town. Ok, let's deploy a solid spinning sidekick (Yoko-geri) to the center mass of this armless DA soldier. Chest kicks work, and down goes this armless asshole. Not so logical now, but in life, logic can be found and lost within seconds of each other.

Time to finish the job and catch up with my Shotokan Warriors. Nice blade cuts from the top down to the combat boots. That's it, the first kill in the year 2026 for the second time around. This alien entity force was snuggled right inside this soldier's liver. Very bizarre location, but nothing shocks me with these aliens. This red-eyed DA was very different from past ones I dealt with. When I say past, I mean the first time I was in the year 2026.

Ok, enough with the time travel bullshit. Crazy, I'm talking out loud to myself again and telling a play-by-play of each thing I'm doing. Why not, it keeps me grounded, and when you're in the terminal realm, who gives a last dragon ass if anyone here's you. Speaking of the last dragon. Got to say it. *Dragonheart* was a cool 1996 fantasy adventure that starred Dennis Quad and none other than Sir Sean Connery. What a smooth, confident kick-ass voice. Think about it. You have a friend who is a dragon, and its voice is Sean Connery.

Ok, enough with past nostalgia of movies. Although I wouldn't mind sitting down and watching DragonHeart right now. Well, I have had a good time, looks like I'm on Route 68 / Sunflower Rd. heading from Daugherty Township towards Pulaski Township. See talking about make believe movies makes this reality easier to take. Plus, it is a good traveling companion. Based on intelligence sent to my

76

optic lens, courtesy of Cool Blue. My SW crew headed towards New Brighton and were able to drift the armored vehicle down Marion Hill Rd. into Pulaski Township, which is just outside the outskirts of downtown New Brighton. It might be a stroke of luck because Zirat Auto Electric is right at the bottom of Marion Hill. Great top-shelf place to get your vehicle fixed, no matter what is wrong with it. Also, the owner is a cool dude that loves fast cars. That being said, maybe my SW unit needs to borrow a couple of those racing cars for the mission. Yep, most definitely a plan to speed things up.

Zirat Auto Electric

Ok, I got a pretty decent running pace going, just a few more feet, and I will pass the Daugherty Fire Hall, which just so happens to be right off of Route 68 / Sunflower Road. If I keep this pace up, I should be at the Zirat repair shop in no time. Oh shit-sandoitchi (sandwich), death has arrived again, but this time the odds are against me on a higher level than I've battled before. Looks like at least 100 DA(s) walking and they are everywhere. They are coming out from every angle around me. Got about a 20 ft distance from them in every direction. No opening to get through them, this is a really a fucked up sandoitchi (sandwich)! Maybe I should have stayed off the main roads, but something tells me that this was a planned encounter. The Old Hive Queen told me she would be waiting in the year 2026, so she must have sent these 100 DA(s) to welcome me with open arms, hands and sharp teeth. Time to prepare my mind and body, because it is Burendo Shotokan time, and kill shots must be accurate and quick. Some creepy-looking DA(s) with an appetite for "The Man Called Clint." int." I guess this is going to turn into a 100-man kumite (Hyakunin kumite), similar to Kyokushin karate. Except, this is to the death.

Here they come, time to start cutting down these corn-stalks of DA death. I got my Han'i Ha" at the six-foot range, Naginata ready, bladed with an extra-long handle. Going to start with a double-hand grip, and then switch to single as I spin in a clockwise circle direction.

Zig zagging through each body of the walking alien dead. Hopefully, with each rotation, I can hit the kill shots. Fuck, it's been 30 minutes into this blood battle, and I've managed to destroy at least 30 DA(s). I guess it's one DA a minute. Crazy, it's like a scene from the 1968 American independent horror film *Night Of Living Dead.* This story introduced flesh-eating walking dead, which would become interchangeable with the word "Zombie." I'm in the house surrounded by the walking dead, and I'm trapped, trying to figure a way out of this dungeon of death and dismemberment. Come to think of it, I did call these DA(s) Corn- stalks of DA death. Makes me think of the 1984 American supernatural slasher film, *Children Of The Corn,* Malachai the leader of the twisted children, would be proud of these Cornstalks of death. Here I go again talking about past memories, and movie mayhem. The strange thing is the DA(s) getting ready to chomp away on me, stopped for a brief moment, and appeared to be listening to me talking out loud about these creepy movies. They must have been a fan of the horror genre, or maybe they are just good listeners. Ok, enough said. I must continue, no matter what.

I keep cutting them down and the DA(s) keep piling up around me like rainbow trout on the first day of fishing. The DA(s) are attempting to climb over the sliced-up DA(s) that are piling up, not good, now they are starting to tumble or jump down towards me.

Decapitation is working, and at least if I separate the head from the body, they lose their compass for a minute or so. This gives a little bit of time to kill-shot the weak point on their body. Fuck!!! This is not good on any level. Trap amongst them, and there are too many moving actively to end me. What a sloppy mess of them scattered and piling up around me. I managed to keep my circle of defense about a 10 ft radius around me, but I am losing ground. Also, these Alien Zombified corpses have the advantage of the high ground. The circle is starting to close in, time to switch to the 4 ft blade range, and utilize Samurai style sword quickly and fast.

Not sure how many I killed, but they keep coming like a waterfall of death. The circle is closing in even more. The last blade range must be used, the 3 ft single handle grip with a double-ended blade cutting weapon for close-range combat.

I must Blade cut fast and true, this is my last chance, and this may be how it all ends for "The Man Called Clint." The DA(s) are starting to fall on top of me as I slice them down with every last bit of my will to survive. This isn't good, because I just got knocked down, and covered over by a blood sea of kill shot DA(s). My hands are trapped, and I can't move my legs to stand back up, I'm fucked, in a really unpredictable way.

80

I can see somewhat through the maze of dead DA bodies, but the hunger is still in full DA form, and these ravenous creatures are trying to get to me through the bodies lying on top of me.

God, only you know the time and the day, I take my last breath on earth, and my next breath among the angels, that's if **God** decides to let me in. If this is the way it is all going to end, I have to say it in the nicest way possible. This is a messed-up dill weed sandwich, please **GOD**? Send me a sign and free me from this hell.

What is that, I see a flicker of silver through the Zombie packages covering my body. I see what looks like a person dressed in silver-covered armor. Not sure if it's a man or a woman but wearing a Japanese *Yoroi* style of Samurai armor. It has a traditional look, but also looks very medieval, and futuristic. For some reason, I think it might weigh a lot less than traditional *Yoroi* armor based on the movement of this Silver coated Samurai. Shit yea!

A sword that looks to be Haja-no-Ontachi (Great-Evil-Crushing Blade).

This sword is the longest in Japan and was donated to the Hanaoka Hachiman shrine in 1859.

This sword is one of a kind and was forged with the wish that it would repel evil and demons, and create a bright, clean, and peaceful society. These are not my words but documented Japanese historical facts. This sword has just been unsheathed, and DA bodies are flying everywhere. Holy Silver Samurai Warrior! This unknown warrior is cleaning the Fucking dojo!!!! The last DA I can see within a distance of my view has fallen.

Ok here we go, I can see the Silver Samurai now, because the fast techniques of death have stopped, and it appears to be a female warrior covered with some DA

81

blood, which is generally the case when the sword starts cutting. Interesting and honorable, this Silver Samurai is bowing her head, almost as if a prayer is being said, out of respect for all of the poor souls she dispatched. I can't explain the feeling that has come over me, I feel like I have a connection with Silver Samurai Warrior, but I just can't figure out where, when or how our roads might have crossed paths before. I will have to take some time to think this out, and when I get a chance to connect my emotions to this moment, I will solve this mystery. I'm just very thankful **GOD** sent me a sign in the form of a Silver Samurai Warrior and when I say Warrior, I mean one ass-kicking alien annihilator. Earth has to be happy she is on the side of good because if she was on the side of evil, the game for survival would be a more deadly event.

The Silver Samurai

   Ok, she just vanished from sight, with no signs of the silver-coated Samurai, she must have left this medieval battleground. How did this Silver Samurai obtain such a unique, and fantastic sword? Also, based on the battle I just witnessed, this sword was retracting down to the length of 3 ft and then extending out to a total length of 15 ft. 15 ft is the original length of the Haja-no-Ontachi. Almost as if this sword was acquired, and then modified with futuristic abilities. Why not, this sword was forged in the EDO period, which was 1603-1868, which is historical Japan. Plus, the high-carbon steel back then was top-shelf tough. No time to invest any more thought in this now, time to get myself out from under this bloody mess of bodies. The Silver Samurai must have moved some bodies from on top of me because I can now move my legs and arms. Ok, I unfucked myself from near death, and it is nice to know violence has a friend. In this case, the Silver Samurai. I don't know who or what this Warrior is, but I am glad she is on my side. Wow, what a nasty covering of DA

83

bodies. There must be at least 200 of them just mangled, and blade cut to pieces.

Time to break out the sanitize kit from my gear bag and clean myself up. Got to make it to my SW team. Based on my optic lens locator, they are still waiting at Zirat's. At least they followed orders and didn't come back to help me.
I'm sure by now they have the exact coordinates of the Hive Queen, or at least Big Boss DA.

Strange? One would think, after that onslaught of Zombie aliens that I just encountered, my body would be exhausted, but for some unexplained reason, I'm ready to kick some more alien ass. I bet this unstoppable endurance and stamina have to do with the Hive Queen's attempt to take me as a host human the first time I was in the year 2026, which ultimately failed. Ok, let's see, I can breathe underwater or underground for that matter, and I now have endless energy that keeps me going. I wonder what other so-called superpowers I will reveal. Time will tell the tale, but I must be firing on all cylinders because I'm talking out loud to myself again, and really enjoying the moment.

Shit what the Holy hellfire is this, it looks to be two more Da(s), those are two creepy-looking Alien DA(s), just standing there looking confused. A bloody mess, and for some reason these two look hungry. They must have been late for the DA frenzy that just took place a little bit ago. Although, they are blocking my path, and seem to be calculating something in their messed-up memory. It is definitely a struggle for a human, when an alien entity gets hold of their brain, and controls their every move.

Well, I guess it's ill shot time again, because I'm going to have to take out these Zombie roadblocks and be on my way. What kind of alien voodoo is this, one of the DAs has positioned himself in a full-blown fighting stance or should I say a back stance (Kokutsu-Dachi). Looks to have 60% of his body weight on the back leg and 40% of his body weight on the front leg. Ready for battle and starting to growl at me like a crazed animal. The other DA didn't seem to be motivated and just collapsed onto the concrete roadway. Yep, that poor human soul couldn't handle the alien entity sucking the life out of him and rejecting the host.

Mmm, I wonder if the DA still standing has taken over a Martial Artist's body and is pulling in memories from his past experience to use against me. I wonder what style of fighting he will bring to this street fight. Alright, it looks to be Taekwondo, which is a Korean style of martial arts. Very effective if a person is correctly trained in the style. Meaning, both sport fighting and street fighting. Time to find out if this DA zombie is a worthy opponent or just got trained by a self-absorbed Sensei. Plus, tons of bullshit martial art schools are out there, and they just try convincing students that they teach the deadliest martial art in the world, as they sit you down to sign up for a lifetime membership.

They convince or bully people into signing a bullshit contract, and they just take your money and even after you sign up for the most expensive training, somewhere along the line, this sneaky Sensei tells you, that for just a little more money, you can get specialized training. What the *Fuck-Training* does that mean, I guess when you were getting trained or taught under the first contract wasn't the best. Those schools are out there waiting to pressure a person or family into signing up for classes. Oh well, back to this Martial Art DA Zombie sizing me up for battle. This fucking thing is going berserk! Looks to be a bloody mess of scraps, but still maintains nice muscle mass. I am about to have a major fight to the Dead Adrenaline death, and he looks like a meat eater! I bet he was a steroid user at your local gym, always trying to get the edge in his training, but never making the sacrifice to gain it through hard work, and by natural means. Even if he did take the natural track in his training, there is nothing natural about him now. This guy is having a heat stroke and wants a piece of me on the dinner plate. Red-eyed, totally aggressive, no remorse left in the tank, only pain and suffering on an alien-zombie level. Going to call this one *Mr. Rage!*

Mr. Rage

Here we go, Mr. Rage is running towards me, and a shifting of weight has commenced, here comes a jumping spinning crescent kick (Dwi-myo dwi bandal chagi) in Taekwondo form. Pretty good height on the kick, but it is a commitment kick, and I don't have time to waste with battling Mr. Rage for too long. Ok, time to counter with a low spinning heel sweep (Gedan Ura-Ushiro-Ashi Barai) to the rear leg of Mr. Rage. Going to tag the first foot of his that hits the concrete first. Wow! Nice recovery by Mr. Rage, who managed to avoid cracking his head on the roadway, and just stood back up. Going to let go of a nice left rear Japanese low round kick (Gedan-Mawashi-Geri) to his outside side knee area, and counter with a left hook punch to the temple(mi) area, and a straight right punch to his right eye socket (Ganka) after those hand hits, I will continue with an arsenal of kicks and hand strikes to end Mr. Rage's anger. Ok this DA can fight, he just avoided the low leg kick, left hook, and straight right, and was able to counter back with two jumps from snap kicks. The second jump front snap kick caught my right shoulder. Mr. Rage had a lot of power behind that kick, and it knocked me back several feet. Luckily, I recovered quickly and launched some kicks of my own. A jump turning roundhouse (tobi-mawashi-geri), a skipping front kick (Sukippu-Mae-Geri), and a spinning back kick (UraUshiroGeri). Landed the jump turning round kick to his right-side neck area, and the skipping front kick to his solar plexus area.

Lastly, another powerful kick crashed into the pelvis area of Mr. Rage, by way of a spinning back kick (Ushiro-Geri). Triple combination kicks work when applied with speed and force. I must have been close to the kill shot with the pelvis ck, because he stumbled back, and has retreated about 6 ft. Looks to have slowed down and paused for a minute.

Mmm, I wonder what he is thinking. Never fails, Mr. Rage just went to the ground and is on his back in an open guard position. Here we go, this Taekwondo guy must have also trained in some form of ground fighting. Now he is waiting for me to come get him, and attack. Typical, this DA can't beat me in a stand-up fight, so he goes to the ground to try his luck. As I have said before, a well-rounded Martial Artist must always have the knowledge and ability to battle on the ground if the fight takes that direction. On the flip side, a well-rounded Martial Artist must have the knowledge and the ability to get back to his feet and stay there. In this case, DA(s) can bite, so the Man called Clint isn't going to be on the menu.

Time to end Mr. Rage's pain and suffering. I should have done this from the beginning, but I'm always looking to test my fighting ability without the use of any type of hand weapon. Rule # 1, never go to the ground when the Dead Adrenaline apocalypse is going down. Rule # 2, never go to the ground when your opponent breaks out a Han'i Ha, at the 4 ft range and blade cuts you into your next life. Yep, never bring a ground fight to a katana blade fight. Mr. Rage, just got his arms removed and feet, time to take off his head, what a bloody mess, but we're battling the Dead Adrenaline apocalypse, so do you think for even one moment this is going to be a pretty outcome.

Nope, it gets ugly and violent, but the only way you can beat these cannibalistic DA creatures is to bring the violence back to them. Ok, the kill shot was located in the pelvis area of Mr. Rage, too late for anger management classes, so I extinguished his rage. Rest in Peace Mr. Rage.

I have to say, for some unknown reason, these DA(s) are more methodical in their violence to a point they understand what's at stake. The Hive Queen must have infused this knowledge of survival into them, they are more violent, but more controlled in how they attack. I'm definitely not sure how she did this, but Alien voodoo is a strong poison of mystery. Another really odd thing, which I never really noticed before, but these red-eyed DA(s) look like they have a set of two right eyes in their head. Must have always been that way, but never really noticed it before. I guess some of these Dead Adrenaline Zombies just get that look in their eyes after the alien takes control of their mind and body. Really weird stuff, but these are aliens from another planet or galaxy.

.

All this talking and thinking out loud is getting me to think about my first time in the year 2026. I remember every moment of the Kumite, Hive Queen, and I fought at the One Strike Karate Dojo. In that battle, she could utilize skills and knowledge from the human shell she took over. Poor Kris was the human, what a warrior, her fighting skills were on full display, even though the Hive Queen did bring in some of her ancient alien-fighting skills, which was no joke. The unusual thing is, up until this battle with Mr. Red Rage, no other DA ever used skill sets from the human prisoner they took over. This ups the game, because if an alien entity can take over a human to the point of even acting like a normal human. This would be a major problem for the human race, but I would think this would take a little time for the DA(s) to be able to do this. I should never underestimate a book by its cover as Master G said, or you miss the first defensive block in a fight. All of this talking out loud conversation with myself has made my road trip to my Burendo Shotokan Warriors go quick, I'm almost at their location.

Fury Ride

Year 2026

Ok, I have made it to Zirat's repair shop, looks like the team is all here. Holy King Author's kingdom. "My Knights of the Dojo" definitely have gotten younger. They looked to have reversed their age by approximately 9-10 years.

"Glad you said that out loud Sir, because we knew we were getting younger, but it was hard to tell amongst ourselves. You know Sensei Clint, how when you are around someone all the time, they gain weight or get older. Kinda sneaks up and isn't as noticeable to the group or people that you see every day. In this case hours are like years. You on the other timetable hand, have been away from us for a couple of hours, so what do you think."

Olivia, and the rest of this wrecking crew, I will say it like I see it. You guys and girls were in the age ranges from 28-29 when we time-traveled our ass's here to the year 2026. Based on what I see before me now; I'm looking at a group of 20- 21-year-olds. Except for Sullivan, he looks like he is still 28 or 29 years old. It's not good when you are now around 21 years of age and look 8 or 9 years older.

On the flip side, when he first arrived in the year 2026, Sullivan looked like he was in his twenties. Sorry, sometimes I get off the track with bad time travel humor.

"You are right Sir; I have always looked older than what my age number says. Genetics' can be a bitch, but I look at things differently, more wrinkles less stress. You see, sometimes people that look younger carry more stress internally, which ages them in a worst way."

Ok Sullivan, not sure if I buy your wrinkled bullshit theory about aging, although this reverse aging thing reminds me of the 2008 movie *The Curious Case of Benjamin Button, starring Brad Pitt.* In this movie, Benjamin Button reverse ages from 84 years old to ultimately ending up an infant baby, which dies. Sounds like a bleak outcome, but just like in this movie. Whether we age forward or in reverse the ending is the same. Death!

My concern isn't the fact you are younger now, but have you retained your skill set of knowledge that all of you acquired, before launching into this mission?

"Ok, that is a very concerning question Sensei Clint, but the answer I am about to give you is going to be one unbelievable bullshit sandwich storm."

Let's hear it Olivia, Time is ticking, and we need to get on the move. By the way, nice bullshit sandwich usage.

"You got it Sir, I ran a check on Sullivan, Oliver, Sandra and myself in reference to brain aging and knowledge retention. The results are staggering, I will go down the list starting with me. Even though I am reverse aging, my mind is not for some unexplained reason. This means that even when I age down to a possible infant stage, I will still have the mindset knowledge acquired at age 29. No more no less. At the infant stage, I will not be able to talk, but I will know and understand that I used to speak if that makes any sense. I will be an adult woman trapped in an infant body. Mmm, yeah this is definitely a terrible thought. Ok, I will continue down the list. Oliver is reverse aging in the same way, except his mindset of knowledge is fading with every second, minute, or hour that passes. Meaning he will formulate emotion and thought patterns for problem-solving according to his reverse age at that time. In an unusual manner, his mind will just disappear, and communication will not be possible when he reaches the

91

infant stage. Basically, his mind knowledge IQ is at the age his body is registering, due to the reverse aging.

Fuck that! My mind is firing on all brain cells. Doctor Olivia, you can take your diagnosis opinion, and shove up your reverse age ass.
No one is going to tell me anything! I got control of this situation, and my mind is sharp as my blade."

"Easy Oliver, Olivia is just giving the life scan facts to each of our outcomes."

"Shut your mouth Sullivan or I will make sure you keep it shut forever!" Hey what the fuck are you grinning and smirking about Sensei Clint!"

Glad you asked Oliver, yep you are definitely acting like a young buck twenty-year-old. Irish Warrior would enjoy talking to you.

"What the hell are you talking about? Listen if you want to go, I can guarantee an ass kicking. Yea, I am 20 years old, and you are just an old man. You ready!"

Now that's classic mistake number one. Never judge a person by what you see. If you do, you will miss the first defensive block in a fight. Come on Oliver, I taught you this teaching, I learned from Master G, see your mind is starting to fade.

"Alright, Man *called Clint*. Get ready, because I am going to kick your ass, and take command of this mission."

("Without hesitation and with lightning speed, power and accuracy. The Man called Clint, sent a vertical punch off his lead left hand, all while side stepping to the outside of Oliver. The punch landed to the right side of Oliver's neck.

92

Placing a massive amount of pressure on the carotid
artery. Just as the left-handed vertical punch landed. A
right handed open palm sword arm strike crashes into the
left side of Oliver's neck, causing pressure and pain to the
carotid arteries on each side. Within seconds, Oliver
collapsed, and was slowly lowered to the ground physically
by the Man Called Clint.")

"Wow!!!! Sensei Clint what the hell just happen to Oliver,
you dropped him like a bad habit."

Well, Sandra, Olivia, and Sullivan. Oliver has become a
liability dill-weed to the mission. His mind is getting mixed
up and can't handle the changes occurring, both physically
and mentally. Time to send him back to the year 2086 by
way of the return time pod. It may work or may not, but if
he stays here, he will definitely die.

"Everyone, Sensei Clint is right."

"What do you mean he is right Olivia?"

"Hear me out Sullivan."

"Every one of us may react differently to the reverse age
effects, meaning this whole process can cause a person to
go insane. Time will tell for the rest of us, but I agree with
Sensei, that we must send Oliver back to the year 2086,
based on the information gathered, using this return time
pod isn't really that advanced. Believe it or not, it's only a
matter of cracking open the time pod and placing it
underneath his back area with him lying on top of it, then
the mechanism of time travel will begin. If **GOD** is willing,
Oliver will travel back to the year 2086, which is the only
year programmed into the time pod. Hopefully, the
command room computer is back online, so he can return
to where he came from. If not, he will come back in the

year 2086, but the exact location of his return could be anywhere in the world."

"Well Olivia and Sensei Clint you are probably correct about Olivier, and his chances of survival if he stays in the past. I agree, send Olivier back to the year 2086."

What is it going to be Sandra girl!

"You know my answer Sensei, send him back. It is the best chance he has for survival. Plus, if Oliver does make it back, maybe he can be of use for the people of the year 2086."

Let's do this then, crack open the time return pod, and place it underneath his back, just between his shoulder blades. Looks like he is lying on his back already based on my carotid artery sleeper strikes. The vertical punch and open-hand sword arm don't always work, but sometimes they work perfectly when applied together.

"Ok Sensei, it should only be a few seconds."

Good to know Olivia, everyone step back from Olivier, because you don't want to be absorbed and encapsulated when this thing launches.

Holy invisible man, Oliver just vanished like a star falling from the sky, except this star vanished traveling upwards.

"Sensei, not to take up any more time, but I would quickly like to tell Sullivan and Sandra the outcome of their reverse aging in reference to their mind."

Yep, go ahead and give them the medical outcome. Then we must get moving, and locate Boss Man, hopefully he hasn't changed into purple eyes yet.

"I will make it quick, and as mentally painless as possible. Ok, Sullivan and Sandra, obviously your bodies are getting younger with every second that disappears. This is a known fact, unlike Oliver, whose mind was younger and fading away. Or myself whose mind isn't getting younger like my body. You two are a completely different outcome and direction when it comes to your mind. Meaning, this is going to sound even crazier than what I've said already. Both of you, Sullivan and Sandra are reverse aging with your bodies, but your minds are getting older instead of becoming younger. Meaning your brain is aging, at a fast rate of deterioration, even faster than Oliver's decrease of brain knowledge.

"Ok, that's not so bad Olivia. We are getting Brainpower that is older and wiser."

"One would think just that Sullivan, but there is an unknown factor involved with both you and Sandra's body getting younger, but your minds getting older. Meaning, eventually your mind will age to a point past what you have existed. When that happens your mind's knowledge will be older than the oldest age you have reached ever in your lifetime.

Meaning this, I do not know if your mind will just go blank or cause insanity. Creepy outcome, but at that point, you will be an infant or, I guess, nonexistent. Time will let us know."

"Geez, thanks for the horrible information, Olivia, but I have to accept it for now. Maybe we can figure out a cure for this reverse age thing. Plus, if I flip out and act like a dill

95

weed, Sensei Clint will put me to sleep, and send me back to the year 2086, which might be a better outcome."

Easy Sullivan, no one is going anywhere. We need to complete this mission, and by the way, you don't have to act like a dillweed to be one.

Sandra, are you good?

"Yep, I'm good Sensei Clint. In a more positive direction, I located the whereabouts of Dill weed Boss Man. I locked on to his location."

Ok, enough said, time to get some transportation to make up some time. This is just what the doctor ordered, fast fury rides for all of us. As Luck would have it, these power machines are just parked here by Zirat automotive. Perfect timing, perfect technique to use at this moment. Let's hot-wire these fury rides up and get to our destination of destiny.

The one with flames on the hood is my ride. Crazy I came from the year 2026 to the year 2086, only to return back to the year 2026, and continue this quest to save humanity by way of transportation from 1950 and 1960's American style motor cars. The Coolness goblet is running over, time to Rock and Roll down the road to our salvation. Burendo Shotokan Warriors pick one of these badass Hot Rods, or should I say Hot Wheels. These vehicles remind me of Hot Wheel cars from when I was a kid, except they are full-size, and are ready for a fury ride.

Sullivan's Vehicle of Choice.

Sandra's Vehicle of Choice.

Olivia's Vehicle of Choice.

The Man Called Clint, Vehicle of Choice.

Running On Empty

Year 2026

Sensei's log, throwing star-date 2026, time is running out, and my Burendo Shotokan Warriors are starting to feel the effects of the reverse age illness. Sickbay is a complicated scenario, Sandra and Sullivan's minds are aging forward, but their bodies are aging backward. Soon their minds will age past existence, and their bodies will be nothing more than a childhood memory. Olivia is feeling the effects of the reverse age illness, but her mind remains the same and hasn't been affected. For the good of the team, Oliver had to be put to sleep and sent back to the year 2086. We are now en route to our intended target, Big Boss Man in hopes of destroying the Hive Queen, who may have already taken over the Big Boss Man's mind and body as a host. Transportation is on our side. We traded in Steel and Wheels for Hot Wheels rolling Thunder down the road. Sensei's log, signing off.

Rolling down the road of pain and suffering trying to make up some time before baby land shows up on my doorstep. Even though, I have lived this tragic dismantling of the human race once before in the year 2026. Something seems different, almost as if we are being guided or controlled by the Hive Queen, and her underlings. I feel like Flash from the 1980 Space opera science fiction film Flash Gordon. He travels to planet Mongo and runs into a villain named Ming the Merciless. In this case, I landed back in the year 2026 on my home planet Earth, which feels like planet Mongo. Either way, the battle continues, and my Burendo Shotokan Warriors are in full battle mode at least for now. Soon they will be running on empty, and then the full weight of this nightmare will be mine again.

Speaking of running on empty, the fuel gauge in this Hot Wheels car is starting to get low. Just rolled onto Route and headed towards Rochester Borough. I bet all the vehicles in this Car cruise are low on fuel. Speaking of car cruises, New Brighton Borough in Beaver County, PA has one of the largest car cruises around. Cool and nostalgic cars show up everywhere. The car cruise people definitely take seriously and bring out some fantastic automotive excellence. Ok, time to get my thoughts back on the road, and focus on our next stop. Just pulled over at the Sheetz gas station in Rochester Borough. Very quiet, no sound or people anywhere to be found. Time to have one of my Burendo Warrior players hack into the gas pumps, so we can fuel up our transportation. You see my Burendo Shotokan Warriors bring some future knowledge like stealing gas in the year 2026. I guess it's not stealing, just borrowing for the sake of our species.

Well, the sun is going down in DA town and I'm starting to hear shrieks of happiness and suffering. Yep, we might have to find a place to hold up until morning. If memory serves me, the first time I was in the year 2026, I waited at my house until day two of this manic nightmare to roll into the morning light of day two. Definitely a good call then and would be now if this damn reverse aging illness wasn't taking time from Sandra, Sullivan, and Olivia's souls.

Olivia, Sullivan and Sandra a choice has to be made. We can find a place to rest and wait until morning or continue through this maze of unknowns. When night falls, the DAs seem to be more active roaming the land of the terminal realm searching for Beaver Countian cuisine, and possibly a human body for host purposes. They take that person over like a puppet in very violent and cruel ways. This will be your call to make. The way I see it, it's going to be a blood bath either way. Talk it over for a minute and let me know. If we do decide to camp for the night, I have the perfect place.

Hold on Burendo Shotokan Warriors!!! 12 o'clock heading our way at full speed, it looks to be a large mass of sorts, lined up side by side about 20 Zombies long. What a Fuck sandwich, it's DA(s) stuck together from their bloody bodies drying, looks to be intentionally done. This sick venue of alien dill weeds is working together like a riot formation of death.

Could it be, that these red-eyed front-line worker DA(s) can understand each other as this formation of pure evil is moving in our direction? Looks to be 50 feet away but is closing fast. No time to race out of here, we still need the gas tanks filled, and we are running on empty.

Ok, SW team, I will take the center, Sandra you take position to the right of me. Olivia, you take the right of Sandra, and Sullivan take the left of me. Spread out and find the kill spots. Han'i Han in hand, blade cut completely through these walking carcasses. Sandra, Sullivan, Olivia you know what you have to do, cut a hole through these DA(s), and get behind them. It is always an advantage when you're behind your attacker. Cut precise and true, we only have one shot at this, or run the risk of getting folded up inside this bloody frenzy. Here it comes, get ready!!!

"Sensei it's moving too fast!!"

Slow your breathing Olivia, focus on the task, control your mindset. In this brief moment, think of something that calms your soul and brings balance.

"I got Sir, just thought of it. Now it's kill shot time!"

Now you're speaking my language.
Olivia!

"Mmm, I wonder what Olivia thought of, because I'm thinking we're definitely screwed if this doesn't work out."

Sullivan, I can hear you talking out loud, that a boy you are embracing all of my teachings. Talk out loud and say it proud.

One last comment, and let the slice and dice party begin, Sandra, are you good?

"Yep, most definitely Sensei! Time to end this walking roadblock of death."

(Three Burendo Shotokan Warriors and their Sensei begin the onslaught of pure blade destruction. Every cut and every technique is completed without hesitation and unshakable concentration. No doubt, no flaws, no interruption, just pure adrenaline to crush the Dead Adrenaline. Nothing is left standing, except the three Warriors and their Sensei. Steam from the blood and carnage rises from the concrete roadway, and the smell of death is undeniable, but the battle for humanity isn't for the weak souled, only for the ones ready to enter this medieval alien octagon of pain and suffering. The night closes in and darkness fills the sky.The sounds of pain and suffering echo through the dark sky from all directions, but an unfamiliar, unrelenting painful cry overpowers the other screams and cries.This sad, hideous, vengeful sound has never been heard by any human being before. Almost as if a mother of her children felt the death of her offspring. What is coming for the three Burendo Shotokan Warriors and their Sensei is not for warriors with a fragile fortitude, but a fortitude of strength. These warriors must wear the pain with courage and without hesitation.)

"Shit! Sensei we're a bloody mess, and what was that nasty scream or cry we just heard."

Well Sullivan, three words. Hive Fucking Queen!!! She is pissed. These 20 DA(s) we just dispersed must have been her immediate family or possibly her actual children if that makes any kind of sense. Based on my past interactions with alien DA(s). She is the mother or top Queen dog that they love and obey. But within this blend of venomous potion, she must have what we call children on Earth. Crazy as it sounds, these alien assholes have feelings, I guess? Fucked up, but why wouldn't it be. Ok, change of plans, we need to take shelter for the night, until dawn early light, because this was only an appetizer of what is waiting in the blood shadows.

"Absolutely Sensei, I agree. We need to regroup and continue in the morning. Plus, this will give me time to try and figure out what is causing this reverse aging bullshit."

Ok, Olivia you're the Master Doctor, so keep looking for an answer.

Sandra, you're going to plan the safest course to a place I know well. Not too far from here, but we need to avoid Hive Queen, and her DA Minions for now, so we can work on a better plan of attack. I figured this out the first time I ventured through 2026, and realized I needed help. In this case, we need help, so we are going to see the one man I know who is still alive. If you haven't guessed who yet, let's just say, he is a technology wizard, IRISH WARRIOR!

"Sensei, are you sure he is alive still?"

Let's see Olivia, I met up with IW the first time around in the year 2026. It was day 2, and if memory serves me, it was around dusk. Based on this, we are a day earlier. I believe IW already has been bitten by one of those DAs, but if we go to his house now, I have no risk of running into myself, which could have dire consequences. Although we must leave by morning and definitely before dusk. As far as explaining, and convincing IW of this manic situation, leave that to me.

Now break out the sanitizer kits, clean up and top off your gas tanks. We need to move now; darkness is upon us, and I'm not just talking about the dark sky of hate. I believe Hive Queen is somehow watching our every move. This Alien bitch is toying with us like a science experiment, and I bet she is giving us her creepy signature smile right as we speak. Ok, SW(s) we're heading to the town of Beaver, my present and past friend IW, doesn't live too far from there.

Plot the course to his house Sandra.

"It's done Sensei, I have to say, you're right about that Hive Queen bitch, it feels like she is trying to roadblock our every move."

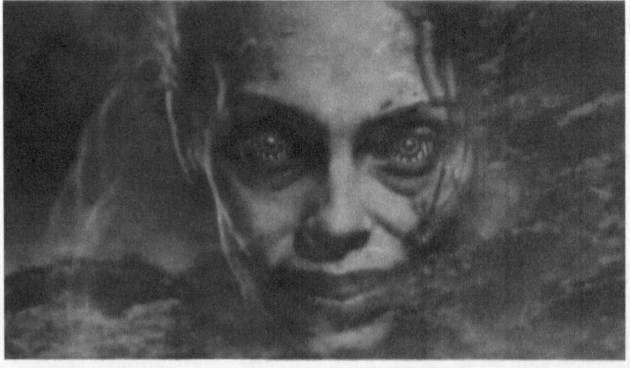

"Sensei Clint!!! There is a large mass floating in the sky, it is hovering right over the Beaver Cemetery. This bizarre-looking mass is moving quickly and zig zagging very fast.

What the hell is that, Sensei? It seems to be waiting in the sky for us to get closer."

Not sure about this one Sandra, Cool Blue, fly up there and see what Science Fiction project is going to rain down on us.

Ok, everyone, Cool Blue is sending back some up-close video footage of the floating cluster in the sky. Shit! It's an unholy swarm of yellow jackets, and they are in pissed-off battle mode.

Bees, why did it have to be Bees? I hate Bees! Actually, yellow jackets aren't bees but are a different species of wasps, which makes this blood swarm even more menacing. Reminds me of my all-time favorite movie, the 1981 action-adventure film Raiders of the Lost Ark, when Indian Jones found the tomb and it was filled with poisonous snakes. Except in my case, I hate these stinging assassins, instead of snakes, although snakes suck too. Last I checked, I was allergic to these winged insects, and based on the video footage sent back from Blue, this flying swarm is definitely infected with DA disease. Obviously, they are being commanded by the Hive Queen bitch!

Well, there's no time to worry, only time to figure out a quick plan of action, because this shit storm is buzzing closer by the second, and I guess their anger is keeping them buzzing.

"Sensei, the readings from Cool Blue indicate that a sasu (sting) from even one of these Yellow Jackets of death will kill a human being instantly. On a positive note, all the data obtained about these DA hosts indicate they take over creatures large and small, but the smaller creatures don't survive, or sustain the entity host very long, and die off. Let's hope that happens very soon Sir."

Yep, that has been the case in my experience, the smaller weaker living organisms can't handle it. Thanks for the update, Olivia, great Japanese usage for sting (sasu) by the way. Now everyone we are definitely in for a very bad outcome, but let's focus our efforts. Burendo Warriors show no fear but maintain total badass focus. You see, this is what Hive Queen wants, needs and craves as she exists in our world. If you give into your emotional fear of hopelessness, she wins, and you lose. There is no middle ground only survival or death, it is up to you warriors to choose because no one can choose for you.

"There is no time to take cover Sensei, so the battle may end here and now."

You are right Sandra, we will make our stand, but we need a distraction or shall I say someone to be bait. Meaning, that if one of us separates from the pack, maybe the swarm will redirect, and go after the human that has broken away from the group. This occurs in the animal kingdom all the time, especially during a feeding frenzy.

Olivia, any life readings on this blood swarm?

"Sir, based on life scan readings, some of the yellow jackets in the swarm are starting to fade, but the bulk of these poisonous flying insects are ready for battle."

Yellow Jackets of Death

"Sensei I got an idea on how to slow down this swarm or possibly distract it, until they die off."

Ok Sullivan I'm up for suggestions, but make it quick, because I'm about to separate from the pack.

"You got it Sensei, here is my thought, I'm going to crash one of our vehicles into that gas station ahead, landing this sucker right into the gas pumps and causing an explosion of sorts, which should send a massive amount of smoke and flames into the air. Based on the savage direction of these yellow jackets, they are heading right for us without any hesitation! Maybe if we time it right, some, or all of the DA swarm will get burnt up or at least confused."

Love the plan, let's do it right now Sullivan!!

"Ok I'm the lead car, so I will let it roll right into the gas pumps, and bail out of my ride, just before impact."

That's the Burendo Shotokan Warrior spirit Sullivan!

"Everyone stay back and let Sullivan make his move because it's either this or death by a thousand sasu(s) (stings)."

"OK Sensei, I'm going, and timing is everything, let's hope this works because if I miss by one second, these killer yellow jackets will sense the danger and pull back."

SW(s) be ready when Sullivan bails out of his ride, we need to scoop him up one way or another and get the fuck out of Beaver Borough. Sandra, you lead the pack, and pick up Sullivan. Olivia and I will make another move to cause any stragglers from the swarm to pick up our trail and follow us. I got an idea to end the rest of these DA-winged insects.

At least we can communicate with each other clearly by way of these optic lenses, which give us the ability to hear and see what the other members of the group are seeing if they choose to communicate back.

Olivia, follow me, we are going to drive past the explosion Sullivan creates in the next couple of minutes. The bulk of the yellow jacket of death should get torched, but some will survive the flames. We will drive past, stop and wait with our engines revving up in a loud mark your territory way. Those DA yellow jackets will be coming for us, so be ready to move, I will stay back, and wait for the winged DA(s) of death to land on and cover my entire vehicle. I will start to drive as this is occurring, but you need to get down by the river, just off of River Road.

You will see me flying past shortly after, and I will not be stopping but making a cannonball jump into the Beaver River with all of the DA Sasu(s) hanging on for dear life. Yellow Jackets don't like water, and given their weakening state of existence, it's going to be a bug bath death outcome.

How will you survive if you go into the river with the vehicle and yellow jacket wasps?"

I guess we'll find out Olivia, but I will say this, to give you hope. The moment I hit the water; I will not drown from lack of oxygen. I'm going to tell you something that only Gordon Scott, Austin Maximillian, and a couple of upper-level doctors, and scientists discovered about me. You see, when I was put into a cationic state of animation by the Hive Queen, which persevered my body and mind, until the year 2086. The purple poison that the Hive Queen gave me to prepare my mind and body to be a host was interrupted and not complete. Anyway, I didn't age, but also gained numerous types of superpowers. One of which is being able to breathe underwater. The rest will remain a secret unless they are needed for this mission to save humanity.

"Wow! Sensei that is unbelievable and extraordinary."

Yep, Olivia, it is some cool-ass superhero shit that is much needed as we speak. Ok, Sullivan, it's moments away from impact with the gas pumps, let's go, he just rolled out of his vehicle and Sandra is a moment away from picking him up. The Hot Wheels car is a second or two from crash and burn and here comes the swarm. Two (NI), One (Ichi) detonation time!!!

(The surround sound of thunder echoes through the air, and smoke and flames erupt from the ground, upward into the sky. Large-size blood pellets of scorched Yellow

111

Jackets sprinkle on the concrete gas station parking lot below.)

"Sensei, Sandra here, do you copy."

Ok Sandra, I copy.

You and Sullivan head towards the Irish Warrior's house. I will meet up with Olivia, who will be waiting for me. We will meet you at IW's house. Just wait and don't go into his house until I arrive.

"Sir, but your vehicle is covered with some of the left-over Yellow Jackets. It looks like a blanket of death attempting to take your life."

I know SANDRA! Thanks for the concern, but I have no time to explain. Keep moving, and I will meet up with you guys when I can.

"Yes Sir, we are enroute to our destination."

THE BREATH OF LIFE

Year 2026

Olivia wait by the shore area of the river on River Road, these savage DA Yellow Jackets are starting to eat through the metal of my vehicle. I will see you in a few. Here I go!!!!

"I copy Sensei!!! **GOD** will be with you, and I will be waiting!"

Time to shift this up a gear and let this Hot Wheel's machine take flight. Here it fucking goes, it's all or nothing. These Yellow Jackets of Death are some scary, creepy-winged DA(s). It's time to end them, oh shit!!! They just entered the vehicle, and they are stinging me! I'm starting to go out, I just hit the water full throttle, and the vehicle is starting to sink. Ok, I'm underwater completely inside the vehicle. My body is burning with the pain from the stings, here it comes, that's it, I'm passing out. Can't catch my breath, has the silent sleep begun?

"Oh, shit sandwich, Sensei Clint do you copy, can you hear me, Clint! It's Olivia, please respond, please Clint! Fuck!!! It's been 10 minutes, and he is still under the water. Come on Olivia, think! Darn, I'm starting to talk to myself like Sensei does. Ok I'm going to attempt to see if video footage is showing up from Sensei's optic lens. Little fuzzy, but it looks like a picture is coming in.

Ok, his eyes must be open, because I can see inside the vehicle, and it looks like a bunch of dead yellow jackets floating around. I can see Sensei hands, and feet floating outward from his body. Let's do a life scan on him, please let there be life. Fuck yes! He is alive but unconscious with a faint heartbeat, and his breathing is shallow. I got to get him out of there, but it needs to be done quickly, and now. Cool Blue fly your upgraded, android-ass down into the water and save your friend. If you understand what I'm asking, give me some sort of sign. Oh, Cool Blue just landed on the hood of my car. He is blue laser lighting something on the windshield. Let's read what Blue has written "Back Up Is Here!" Cool Blue just launched from the hood of my ride and spiked himself into the river. Go Blue, Go! Save him the world needs the Man called Clint."

(Cool Blue enters the river's darkness and locates the wreckage of the Hot Wheels vehicle at the bottom of the river's bed. The entire vehicle is covered with a glue-like substance of dead bloody Yellow Jackets, without hesitation Blue extends his left hand, and what looks like a torch-type cutting tool pops out from Cool Blue's top portion of his metal hand. A large hole is cut into the top of the vehicle, inside is the Man-called Clint's lifeless body secured somewhat by his seatbelt. Blue enters the vehicle and removes the seatbelt. Sensei Clint's body starts to float upwards out of the wreckage, Cool takes a swimming flight underwater, and picks up some speed, strikes Sensei Clint's body from the back and pushes him up to the surface. Upon breaking the surface of the river water, Cool Blue grips the right wrist of Sensei Clint with both of his tiny, but strong android hands. Suddenly, Cool Blue takes flight with Sensei, he is flown over to Olivia, and placed gently onto the ground.)

"Ok Blue, I'm going to do a health check to see what damage his body sustained. His breathing is getting stronger, and for whatever reason there is no water in his lungs. Also, it appears from the life health scan, Sensei Clint was stung over 200 times by those killer Yellow Jackets of death, but the strange thing about it is his body is absorbing the wasp venom with no signs of allergic reaction. Meaning he is absorbing the positives of the stings, but none of the negatives. That means I don't have the data, but it means he should survive. Sensei's heart is getting stronger by the second and looks to be recovering. Cool Blue, help me get Sensei Clint into my vehicle, we need to get out of here and head to his friend's house. Hopefully, Sensei Clint wakes up, before I arrive at this guy named Irish Warrior's place because he sounds like a person who doesn't take kindly to unknown people.

"SENSEI WAKE UP! Wake up Sensei Clint"

Olivia, I can hear you loud and clearly. Wow! What a ride on the edge of death. Man, those Wasp stings hurt like hell, the crazy thing is at this very moment I feel extremely energized and ready for battle. I have to say, just as I started to sink to the bottom abyss of the river, and the deadly DA Yellow Jackets were starting to enter the vehicle, I thought for a split second my death was going to be a very painful and lonely one. Even though, when death does come knocking, it can be a solo or possibly non-solo event, if you believe in **GOD,** and his laws then you will be good to go. The funny thing is, I didn't feel **GOD** around me totally, not like when Hive Queen almost took me out before. But **GOD** was definitely there, and I even spoke to him. Maybe he knew I had a couple of angels on earth, one human and one made of metal. Yeah, that's right, I am talking about you and Cool Blue. You were my savors on this day of battle. Cool Blue has always been there for me, even from the very beginning, but now I know without a doubt you will not flinch under pressure, and battle on to save me, and humanity for that matter. Thanks, and remember no matter what happens, I will make sure you survive, Olivia.

"Well, geez Sensei, I thought you were a goner, and no matter what, I got your back too. If it wasn't for you, all of us would be dying back in the year 2086. Plus, you are my teacher in this twisted alien-infested world, and we need you to keep on kicking if you know what I mean."

You need me to keep on kicking, now you're speaking my language, Olivia. Ok, we are getting close to Irish Warriors House.

Here I go again Olivia, but it's the way I'm programmed, and I'm going to say it. I mentioned sinking under the water into the abyss, and thinking for a split second this was going to be a painful, and lonely death. Well anyways, it makes me think of the 1989 movie *The Abyss,* starring Ed Harris and Mary Elizabeth Mastrantonio, where humans were facing many dangers, and encountered aquatic aliens. Also, the 1992 movie *Split Second,* Rutger Hauer, and Kim Cattrall, where it was discovered what they might be hunting might not be human.

Ok Sensei, wow you are a little out there, but I love it, and like that you said it keeps you going. By the way you're not going to believe this, but I happened to have seen both of those movies, it was archiving oldies at the Super-screen theater in at the Future City outlet Mall. I actual liked both movies."

Good stuff Olivia, ok looks like we have arrived at Irish Warriors house, and there is Sullivan, and Sandra waiting, just up from IW's house.

How is it going, are you both still in one piece?

"Well Sensei, both Sullivan and I almost bit the death dust, on our way to Irish Warriors' house. You see, we encountered two very hungry DA(s), and they tested our skills on a different level. Sullivan and I had to outsmart and outfight these savages with more awareness and fewer techniques.

116

"What went down in DA town Sandra."

"Olivia, it wasn't a pretty outcome, and the blood fest was on full battle display."

"Yep, Olivia and Sensei Clint, this was a real messed up Fuck salad sandwich!"

Ok Sullivan, so it was a little bit healthy, but a lot unhealthy.

"You could say that, Sensei."

Shit, we don't really have time for this, but now I need to hear the story of what happened.

"Ok Sensei and Olivia, let's have Sandra tell this twisted tale that will really make you understand the complexities of these evil alien A-hole invaders."

"So, we left you and Olivia in the town of Beaver, hoping that the Yellow Jackets of death wouldn't become a permanent jacket on you Sensei. Upon heading towards Irish Warriors' house, we encountered two very unusual, freaky-looking DA(s). They were standing in the middle of the roadway, just waiting for us to run them over with our Hot Wheels vehicle. There was no movement, just a death stare in our direction from both of these carnivores' animals. Sullivan's vehicle was rolling over and both Sullivan and I were able to jump out of it before it came crashing down. Then it happened, both of these crazy DA(s), relentlessly started to smash and attack the Hot Wheels ride."

"They beat on the steel and wheels until nothing was left, but a flattened cube of steel. It almost looked like it went through a trash compactor, except large and small chunks of flesh, along with a massive amount of blood, covered the steel cube. I mean it was a splatter fest of carnage, after this was completed both of the DA(s) quickly looked directly at Sullivan and I with a look of total complete hate.

Then these alien DA(s) pointed at us and uttered these words "No More!" Within those seconds both Sullivan and I realized that a shit sandwich was about to come our way."

Biker DA Dudes

"I could be wrong, but I believe these DA(s) might have been in a biker gang because they both had leather jackets on and worked as a team. You see, I read about bike gangs that existed back in your day, which were very interesting groups that were known to be very violent in nature but did have a code. One of these codes did involve protecting their own. In this case, these two definitely had each other's back and we're going to fight to the death. At that moment Sullivan and I got prepared to battle these DA(s), and knew we had to stop them with only one kill shot a piece. You see after witnessing the steel and wheels being twisted and smashed into a steel cube, our bodies were no match for that type of impact. Plus, our minds were not as sharp, due to the reverse age bullshit, so we needed to end this battle with fast action. Then this thought somehow entered both of our minds, to look for an area on the Biker DA(s) bodies they were protecting. Suddenly it appeared to us, both of these DA(s) were guarding the left upper side of their abdomen, which happens to be the spleen area.

All that was left now was to pick a technique to totally destroy this area, which needed to be deployed at close range to make sure the attack lands exactly on the spleen area. At that moment, Sullivan and I knew what technique needed to be used to end each of these DA(s). We went with an unexpected commitment technique that you (Sensei) taught us. The spinning upper-cut elbow strike (Empi-Uchi), will cut upward, right underneath the rib cage, and if launched correctly the opponent will never see it coming until his spleen explodes. One chance, no choice, either it works, or it's lights out for us. both of the Biker DA Dudes were moving in very cautiously as if they knew something was up. Then with an unexpected leap, both of these DA(s) decided to come in for a bite. At that very second, Sullivan took the DA on the right, and I took the one on the left. Perfect timing, speed, power, and most importantly accuracy. Both of our elbows landed right on the kill shot target and dropped the Biker boys like they never existed. I guess extinction has awakened, but not for us on this day. Anyways, Sullivan and I landed the spinning upper-cut elbow with such power that both of the spleens belonging to the Biker DA dudes exploded, and when I say exploded, I mean blood went everywhere. These DA(s) were extremely powerful, but apparently, their skin and

119

muscle were slowly melting away. On a side note, our weapons of choice were crunched up in the Hot Wheels cube that these DA(s) destroyed, so no hand weapons could be used, except for a few throwing stars attached to our uniforms, along with a couple throwing knives. These weapons might have worked, but sometimes you just got to test out your Burendo Shotokan skills to keep sharp, like I've heard you say many times, Sensei."

Biker DA(s) Bit the Death Dust!

Fantastic job Sullivan and Sandra, you made the right choice, because both of you are still here kicking. Top-shelf Burendo Warrior stuff, given your reverse age illness situation. Also, now that these DA(s) are starting to speak English, which is a step up, on the evolution chart. They are becoming smarter and more methodical about how and when they attack. All of us must be more aware of this when we battle the Alien dill weed DA(s).

Ok team, we need to be smart about this, and not cause a bad reaction from Irish Warrior, because I don't believe you would like the outcome. I want you all to stay back for a moment, Cool Blue, and I will attempt to make contact with IW. According to our day data, it is the first day of the DA take over, so IW has already been bit by a DA, and the slow death of the blood infection has started for him. Plus, by the half-eaten dead human bodies scattered around in massive pools of blood, the DA(s) were here, but left to head to the Fracking/ Cracker plant. The first time I met up with Irish Warrior in the year 2026, it was the second day of the alien invasion, and if memory serves, IW was fighting off some DA(s) and got chomped on by one, luckily for him the Hive Queen was calling her DA minions to the Fracking / Cracker plant to nest up in a humongous blood worm mass, so all the DA(s) left.

Time to make first contact with IW, Blue buzz over to his front door and give a little knock. After you knock on the door, fly up above the house and wait, because you're going to want to see this. Wait for it, here it comes, the front window is sliding open, and a metal canister has just shot out of the window, and now it is rolling onto the ground. Get ready in two seconds, Cool Blue you're going to get to meet your robot self from the year 2026.

Pow! Here comes Cool Blue 2026, the original ass-kicking android.

Cool Blue 2086, it's time to introduce yourself to yourself, if that makes any type of time travel bullshit sense.

Fly on down there Cool Blue 2086, and say hello to your past self, which is Cool Blue 2026 from this year. Now this is something I will never ever see again, two Robots from different times, one from the future, and one from the past, both are connected by the same internal memory bank, even though the external metal shell has changed.

121

I'm going to get some popcorn for this one because I'm not exactly sure how this is going to go down in DA town. It might be a mistake to have these Robots meet like this, but what the hell, let's see how it goes.

Cool Blue 2026 (AKA: CB2026)

Cool Blue 2086 (AKA: CB2086)

The meeting of the Bot minds has commenced, interesting to watch both of them communicate with each other with a data conversation. I'm not sure what that looks like, but CB2026 and CB2086 just gave each other a Keii o motto unzuka (respectful nod) of understanding like two Samurai warriors knowing what they are about to face.

Ok, Burendo Shotokan Warriors, it is time for me to meet my old friend Irish Warrior, hopefully he is in a good mood and doesn't think I'm going to crazy town when I tell him, I'm from the year 2086.

Holy Shit! Irish Warrior just came outside his front door and looks to be limping slightly. Damn DA bite definitely happened already, and the infection is starting to work against him. Irish is giving a look of confidence, and interest. Almost as if he knows something and can't wait to give the information.

Irish Warrior

Irish, I came back in time to save humanity from this horrific invasion. One day from today my present / past self will show up at your house for help. You will send Cool Blue outside, like you did today, but Blue will give me a code set of words, which will be laser imaged into my Steel and Wheels windshield if that makes any sense.

"Really, ok Clint, if this is true, what three code words would Blue use."

'What About Your Rights!'

"You're wrong Einstein!"

I'm wrong, what kind of bullshit response is that IW.

124

"HAA! Easy Clint, I already know what's going down in DA town. You see Cool Blue 2026 gave me the low down on current events from the future, if that makes sense. I have a computer program that played back the data conversation Blue-2026 and Blue-2086 were having. Sorry, I was just screwing with you to see if Clint 2086 is fast on his feet like Clint 2026."

Good one IW, messed up, but comical. Now you're giving me another nickname, like I have said, you are a technology Genius.

"This is true Clint, now come inside, and bring your Warriors with you".

"Wow Sensei, your right about Irish Warrior, he doesn't like stupid people."

To be exact Sandra, he was even making sure I didn't become stupider by this Time Travel shit. I love it, that's why we're friends, he is always reshuffling the deck to get a better hand. Ok, you heard the man, let's go inside. "Ok, Burendo Shotokan Warriors, you can put your gear bags down here and take a load off. I bet you are all pretty worn out and need some food and beverage."

"Thank you, Sir, we appreciate this and are in much need to refuel our bodies."

"Mmm? What's your name young lady."

"My name is Olivia and I'm the Doctor on this mission."

"Ok, so she is Olivia and who are the other two people."

IW that would be Sandra and Sullivan, Sandra's my expert in navigation / survivalist in any type of terrain. Sullivan is my lead Scientist on this mission. Obviously, if

125

they showed up with me, I trained them in the way of Burendo fighting.

"Ok, good to know Clint, now what are we going to do about these invading creatures."

Well Irish Warrior the plan is to locate the leader (Hive Queen) and take her out. If we are lucky, we can kill her, before she is made even more powerful from a set of floating jellyfish blood masses.

Floating Jellyfish Blood Masses

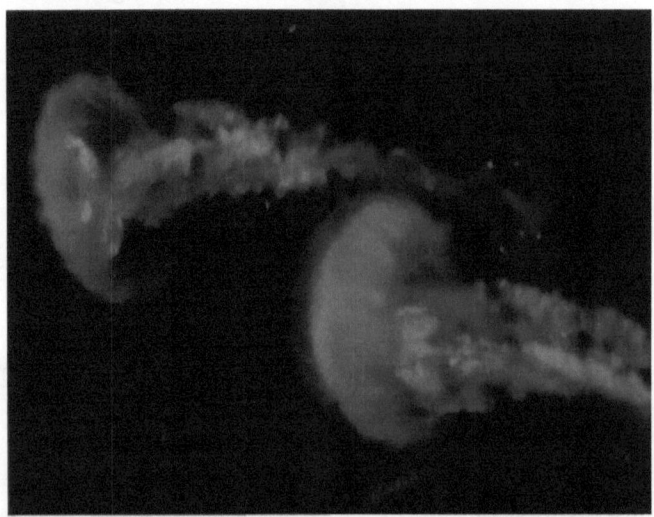

I'm going to have to give you the low down about who, or what Hive Queen is, and how to kill this entity, and her DA human eating front line workers. By the way Irish Warrior, DA stands for Dead Adrenaline, a name I gave these vicious alien invaders. This is crazy, I've already told you this stuff, the first time I was here, but it was told to you tomorrow, over 60 years ago by my past self, if that make any kind of real sense. This time travel shit is one wild ride, but we're on the ride now, so let's enjoy it.

"Yep, you're right Clint, it's hard to believe your other self is here in the year 2026, but the future self is standing before me from 2086. This is a lot to take in, but I do believe what you're telling me is true, because who the hell shows up at my house with a future robot that flies, along with Burendo Shotokan Warriors. I will tell you who, Clint 2086!"

Now that's a good one, giving me a nickname like the two Cool Blues.

"Ok Clint, time to go over what information you have gathered from the year 2026, to 2086, then back to the year 2026."

OK, I got an idea IW, I'm going to speed this briefing process up, Cool Blue 2086, tell Cool Blue 2026 the major details about this take over on American soil, and how it affects the past, present, and future. IW, use some of that fancy bullshit sandwich computer playback stuff you got from Cool Blue 2026 earlier but go in another room to watch and listen because I don't want to relive any of those moments again. Plus, with a friend like you, who needs enemies, especially when I came all this way from the year 2086, just to have you become the dill weed of technology.

Now that's funny, I definitely know it's you Clint, ok, I will take some time to get up to speed on these past, present, and future events."

Ok, while IW is in the other room catching up on the DA town's past, present, and future events. How is it going to find a possible cure, or at the very least, slowing down the reverse age issues you guys are suffering?

Also, I need to know how you are holding up mentally, Sullivan and Sandra, because unlike Olivia, whose body is getting younger with every hour, she still has her mental faculties that are aging at a normal rate forward. Unlike both of you, who are mentally getting older, but your body is getting younger.

"I got nothing on that front of information that could be helpful. Also, I'm starting to forget things that I have learned, or were taught to me. It is hard to focus, remembering some of the simplest things has become a confusing task."

It's not good to hear that Sullivan, but it's better to let all of us know, so we can figure out a solution.

Sandra, what about you, how are you doing?

"Honestly, about the same, in fact, I believe I need a set of glasses to see better. Both my far and near sight are hot. Not a good thing when it comes to navigation, this is one big fucked up age related sandwich."

You're right Sandra, no one could train, or prepare for such a bizarre medical problem that has afflicted this team.

"Well Sensei, my mind is firing in the correct fashion, obviously my body is getting younger at every moment.

In fact, the reverse age thing is even worse than I thought originally. The process is moving faster than I predicted earlier. This means that by tomorrow morning, I will look like a 7-year-old girl, even though my mind will be of the age of a 28-year-old woman. I do have a couple possibilities to stop this type of metamorphosis, but I seem to be missing a valuable piece of data, I just can't find this piece. Going to keep running medical scans on us and see if I can get lucky."

Sounds like a plan Olivia, in the meantime, everyone get a couple of hours rest, which might help your minds in some way. Set your timepieces to wake up in a couple of hours.

FIND PEACE WITH THE FUTURE

Year 2026

Ok, time to wake up Warriors, you all must have been very tired, because none of you even heard your time piece alarm going off. Nap time is over kids, we need to gather our thoughts, and move forward with this mission.

" Hey Clint, I just got done with the movie of the week, and that was a really fucked up grim-reaper ride of information."

I know it really is some messed up stuff Irish, you have to see it to believe it.

"Yeah, now I know how these DA Alien Zombies can bite the dust, and that your team is starting to deteriorate from this unknown reverse age shit. Also, how I will eventually die from the alien poisonous bite given to me by one of those DA's. Pretty negative outcome to say the least, but based on the fact you and your team are here now. We can change the outcome of the future, which may be for the better or the worse.

My thoughts on this shit sandwich, is to reshuffle the deck and make a new sandwich that just might taste better."

Exactly IW, that's why we're here, and I knew you would put perspective on this sad state humanity is suffering. It's time to focus our knowledge, and understanding of the current events, and give it a noticeable kick in a different direction. No more worrying about what may happen in the future, based on how we react in this year 2026.

"Sensei Clint, I have some useful information that just may be the key to stopping this reverse age thing, and bring Sullivan, Sandra, and I back to our normal original state. While everyone was sleeping, I ran a life scan on each of us, and it resulted in some very positive feedback."

Ok, spill the beans Olivia, because the clock of life is ticking, and for some it seems to be moving even faster for.

"This is so true, ok so Sullivan, Sandra, and I all arrived in this year of 2026, not ever having been in his time and year before. Every moment we are in this past year, our bodies are rejecting the surroundings.

We don't belong here, because we never existed in the past.

This is why we are having major issues with our body's life span. Basically, our mind and bodies are confused, and not in balance with our internal life clock. This clock needs reset or recalibrated, so our mind and body understands and accepts the year we're living in."

"Wow! I have to say that makes perfect sense to me because I have existed in the year 2026 already, so my mind and body had no problem with my internal clock. Crazy interesting break down Olivia, but now we need to figure out a way to reset the clock."

"I have a possible idea that is really radical in nature but could be the missing piece, or solution to this medical puzzle of pain and suffering."

Let's hear it Irish Warrior, because time has just gone to warp speed for my team, because based on what I see before me right now. Olivia's guesstimating timeline for the reverse age disease might be not exact. Take a look.

"Wow! Is it me or did we just let in a couple of youngsters that are 7-8 years old."

I know this is some crazy stuff IW.

Olivia, Sullivan and Sandra, you guys just totally decreased in your physical appearance, which happened within moments of speaking with you. Irish Warrior and I are now standing here looking at three young children, but we know it is you. The only positive thing about this is the state-of-the-art futuristic combat uniforms you are all wearing are made of a material that changes to the size you are no matter your height, weight, or age. Really cool, at least this is one thing the future 2086 got right, clothing that changes with your age, height or weight. Someone must have made a mint on that invention clothing idea. Gordon Scott was telling me about this back in the year 2086 when they were designing bite-proof uniforms. At the time, I didn't really understand why Gordon told me this about the uniforms, but now it makes me wonder if he knew something about the reverse age thing and its effects on the Burendo Shotokan Warriors. Sorry, I got a little reverse nostalgic about the future, if that makes sense. At least you kids will fit in your combat uniform.

"My voice might sound very young, but my mind is the same Sensei, unfortunately for Sullivan and Sandra that isn't the case, based on how their physical body got younger, but their minds are aging at a rapid rate. Also, the onset of possible age-related memory loss and confusion has set in."

Olivia

I see and hear what you're saying Olivia, both Sandra and Sullivan have a blank look going on that could be described as being Zombified. Given the state of Beaver County, we don't need any more Zombies running around.

Sullivan   **Sandra**

"Wow Clint! This is some crazy ass Sci-Fi stuff going on right before our eyes. One minute they were roughly 18–19-year-olds, and suddenly they transformed into children. Very interesting, and sad at the same time. It's one thing to be getting younger, but when your body is getting younger, but your mind is aging at a fast rate, that is a whole other mindset of cruelty for Sullivan and Sandra.

On the flip side, most people would think that Olivia's got a better deal, due to the fact her mind is maintaining its original age. Right at this moment, maybe she is better off, but in the not-too-distant future, she will have the mind of an adult trapped in the body of an infant. Anyways, when this reverse age disease runs its course, only God knows the outcome for these poor souls."

Ok, Irish what is the possible cure for this reverse age shit that you just mentioned to us.

"It's a long shot to take, but here's what I'm thinking Clint. If we let Olivia, Sullivan, and Sandra get bitten by one of those Dead Adrenaline Zombies, just a little bite. The shock of the bite, along with the alien virus entering their bloodstream. Internally they will start to fight back with fear, anger and sadness. This will give them a shock in their mind and bodies. Just as this is occurring, each one of them will be injected with your blood. Meaning the Man called Clint's blood will be given to them. At that very moment, hope will become their most important emotion. Think about it Clint, your body and mind responded positively when you were stung by an uncountable number of yellow jackets. Your body healed fast, and any issues mentally or physically you had going on got better. This only happens after a major event attacks your mind and body.

Based on this, if we give these three youngsters a dramatic painful event, and inject them with your blood, which will fight off the virus, and reset any physical or mental issues going on inside their body. As Olivia said, reset their internet clock. On a side note, if you haven't already figured it out by what I have been saying. I just found a cure for the DA blood virus going on in my body from getting bitten already. Let's test my hypothesis on me, if I'm cured by your blood, then these Burendo Shotokan Warrior kids are next to try. No dramatic event is needed for me because when you realize your dying that is enough to shock anyone's system."

Let's do this Irish Warrior, no more time to waste.

Olivia, are you ok to give the blood injection?

"Yes Sir, no worries, no problem. I will take some blood from you and inject it into Mr. Irish Warrior. Ok, the blood injection is completed Sensei Clint."

135

Thanks Olivia, stand back everyone, because we don't know how Irish Warrior is going to react. This could be very violent or not, but we will see.

(Irish Warrior starts to violently shake, and gasp for oxygen, his eyes close shut for a second, then slowly open wide, as his body begins to erupt into a distorted tremor that matches the speed of a hummingbird's wing movements. The naked eye attempts to follow these movements of pure power but cannot. Irish Warrior is like a moving blur that can't be focused in on, and suddenly without warning the violent movement stop, and Irish Warrior is left unconscious lying lifeless on the floor.)

Olivia, run a life scan on Irish, see if he is going to make it, and if the Alien blood poisoning is gone.

"Doing it now Sensei, ok his life scan is normal, and no signs of the alien blood infection. All of his vitals appear to be normal, and Irish Warrior should be waking up. Ok, Irish Warrior has been cured of the Alien blood infection, which is really good, because I thought he might be a goner, Sensei."

How do you feel Irish Warrior, according to Olivia's life scan check, you appear to be healthier now than before you got bitten by one of those red eyed Dead Adrenaline Zombies.

"Well Clint, I feel really good, almost as if I'm in a place of peace, calmness, and nostalgia. Also, I have love for family, friends and **God,** which matters the most, and the rest is just Bullshit. I just can't explain it."

Ok Ha Ha, Irish Warrior is back, because he is busting my chomps, which only IW can do with such precision and believability. Good one Irish.

"Wouldn't have it any other way, Clint. Ok, I think it's time to cure these Burendo Shotokan Warrior youngsters before t's too late."

Exactly, Irish Warrior, now we need to find a wondering DA straggler who isn't with a large group of his cannibalistic friends. I know just the place to find a DA walking around by herself. The place is right in front of the One Strike Karate Dojo in Monaca, there should be one of the laziest DA human hosts to ever exist. This would be the "Cleaning Witch", she will become very violent, but only after you provoke her enough to switch on the motivation to attack. I dealt with her the first time I was here in DA town.

The Cleaning Witch

Ok, Irish, and kids, let's take a short road trip down to Monaca, it's only about 10 minutes or so away.

"I think we need to get going Clint, because Sullivan, and Sandra are on a downhill slide to major memory loss, and deterioration."

Yep, you're right Irish, hopefully, this bite and blood thing works on them, because if it doesn't do the trick, our next option might have to be the Health Hut. Going to need to get some vitamins, minerals and everything organic, and in between in their system. What better place than a top-shelf business like the Health Hut. If memory serves me, the Health Hut has two locations, one in Chippewa Township, and Beaver Borough. Great products, and a fantastic family-owned business. No doubt about it, the Health Hut might be able to bring back the blue skies above, instead of this dark cloudy sky, which isn't healthy at all. Mmm, "Health not Hate" Catchy slogan if I do say so myself. Sorry getting lost in the health sauce again, keeps my mind healthy if you know what I mean.

"Good one, I understand Clint, but we need to go now."

Ok, Irish let's load them up, we're going to the town of Monaca. Cool Blue 86, fly ahead, and scout out the area in Monaca, see if Cleaning Witch can be located.

HEALTH HUT

HEALTH HUT 2

Ok, we just made it into the town of Monaca, and based on optic information sent back from Blue 86. Cleaning Witch is hanging out right in front of the One Strike Karate Dojo, just like last time I was here. Blue 86, cause a little distraction, and fly passed Cleaning Witch a couple of times. While you are doing this, Irish will release Cool Blue 26 that just happens to be with us for the fun. Cool Blue 26 is going to give Cleaning Witch a tackle of sorts that will knock her down on the ground. Once she is down, both of your android battle machines are going to hold each of her arms down, at which time Irish, and I will bring Sullivan, and Sandra over to the Cleaning Witch's nasty mouth / teeth, going to let the Cleaning Witch take a little nip at Sullivan, and Sandra. They won't understand, and will be really scared, but it has to be done.

Olivia, just wait in the vehicle, until we get these two bitten by the Cleaning Witch. I will come to get you once it is done. You will need to inject some of my blood into both of them as quickly as possible. You know what, I must be slipping, you need to be right next to us Olivia, meaning as soon as they are bit, inject them with my blood.

Yes, Sir Sensei, I will be ready with the blood I have taken from you earlier.

You ready Irish Warrior!

"Let's do this as quick as possible, because they are fading fast, and Olivia is getting younger by the minute Clint."

_ Time to move, the Cleaning Witch just got knocked over courtesy of Cool Blue 2026. Damn I never realized how fast Cool Blue can run and hit. One powerful android to say the least, really good technique by the way. The Witch bitch is down, and the android twins got her secured.

140

"Shit Sullivan is getting pissed off, and scared Clint. He is really confused, and just doesn't understand, but who would, he is about to get chomped on by one nasty ass DA. Here it goes, I will try to get this done quick. What the fuck, the Cleaning Witch won't bite Sullivan arm, she doesn't seem interested."

Exactly Irish Warrior, what the fuck! Yep, some things never changed, still lazy ass dill-weed.

Time for plan B, Cool Blue 26 and 86, when I give the signal let the Cleaning Witch up off the ground. Get ready, because she is about to get pissed off. When Cleaning Witch flips out, and starts moving our way, she will be looking to get a bite out of someone. It's going to have to be Sullivan, and Sandra, then Olivia.

Olivia, the plan has changed, you will be getting bitten, along with Sandra, and Sullivan. Irish will administer the blood injections.

"Ok, Sensei!"

"Irish Warrior here are the blood vials of Sensei's blood, along with the syringes. It will only take a drop or two. Not much is needed to fight the blood infection, along with the reverse age bullshit."

"Thank you, Olivia, no worries, everything is going to be alright."

Time to Clean the Fucking Dojo! Let the Cleaning Witch up Cool Blue brothers.

Now wait for it, she will go psychotic any moment now, be ready it happens very fast.

Oh shit!!! Cleaning Witch is definitely hungry!

Hungry Cleaning Witch

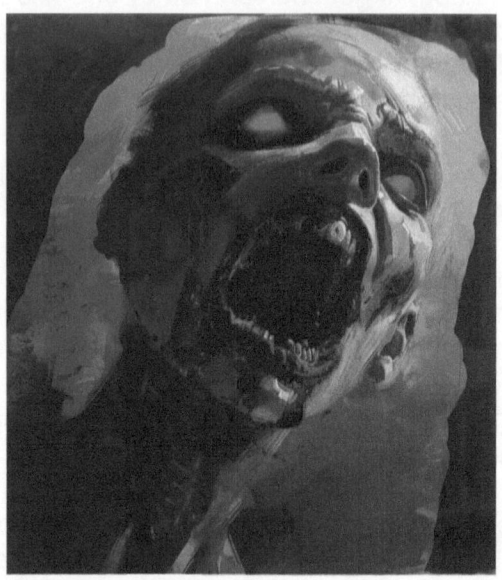

(The Cleaning Witch lets out a high-pitched scream of suffering and pain. The taste of human flesh is unquestionably the reason for today's hunt. Happiness overwhelms her as she moves closer and closer to her prey. Without warning, the Cleaning Witch is adjacent to the sad pathetic humans, but not on this day. The prey is waiting to be bitten, which is part of the cure in this upside down world.)

Let's do this Irish, the Witch bitch is here, move quickly with Sullivan, and let her take nip at his upper forearm. Nice technique Irish, now move back, and give the blood injection. Go place, Sullivan back in our vehicle, I will hold off the Cleaning Witch, until your quick return Irish.

Ok, I am back Clint!

Just in time, she is really going berserk, must be extremely hunger, and is pissed because you took her meal away Irish.

Ok, Olivia, bring Sandra over here and let Irish take her. Same as before, nice forearm bite, blood injection, place in the vehicle. You will be next Olivia, so get ready.

Yes Sensei, ready to go.

The deed is done, Sandra has been bitten, and has got the blood injection, and placed back at the vehicle.

Your next Olivia, so get over here fast. Oh no, Cleaning Witch, just decided to make an unorthodox movement around me, and is plotting a course straight towards the vehicle with Sullivan, and Sandra. The only person between the plate of food, and her is Irish.

Going to try to catch up to her, but this one's going to be up to Irish Warrior, because the Cleaning Witch is like a spider to a fly.

Irish Warrior! You have got to stop her before she reaches the vehicle.

I got his Clint! One thing I hate more than young bucks is lazy ass people. It takes an alien infection on a massive scale for a lazy person to have a goal and get motivated. The goal is feeding on humans, what a messed up double-shit sandwich.

(Irish Warrior reacts with unexpected speed, and swiftness deploying a Pendulum Mid-Level kick (Furiko Chudan geri) inside kick (Yoko-geri) form to the hip area of the Cleaning Witch, knocking her down to the ground like a kite falling from the sky. The Cleaning Witch, becomes very

143

upset, and spasmodic, while attempting to get up off the ground.)

Yes! What about your rights! Nice technique Irish Warrior, I see you have been practicing some of the techniques that were taught to you by me from back in the day.

"I have somewhat, but I have to say the Dragon Slayer blood I was injected with that cured me, appears to have improved my fighting techniques. Thanks Clint."

Ok Olivia, stay next to me, we're going to let Cleaning Witch take a small bite on your arm, as she trying to recover, and get up from the ground.

Sensei, my arm just got a decent bite from the Cleaning Witch.

Irish! Give me the Dragon Slayer blood (Aka The Man Called Clint's blood), I will inject myself.

"You got Olivia, here you go."

Let's move people, the Cleaning Witch just got her deteriorating body back upright, and she is really off the charts with anger, and hate. I have to say, this is even more vicious than I've ever seen coming from this lazy shit sandwich.

"Ok Clint, let's get the hell out of here!"

Exactly Irish, you can drive.

Wait a second, where did Olivia go. Oh shit, it looks like she is running towards the Cleaning Witch at full tilt. Still a small little girl with an adult mind heading towards pure evil. I hope there is a good reason for this, because we're about to find out.

"Wow! Clint that was an amazing kick, which almost took the Cleaning Witch's head off her body, talk about reverse whiplash."

This is so true Irish, which makes sense because my past self completed a nice spinning wheel or heel kick (UraUshiro-Mawashi-Geri) on the Cleaning Witch, which just so happens to take her head off her body. I thought it was because of her rotten body, but now I know Olivia's kick started the detachment. Good for her.

"Ok, Sensei we can go now, I just took care of the problem."

You most certainly did Olivia.

"What can I say Sensei, throat kicks work. I went with the Yoko-Tobi-Nodo-Geri (Flying-Side-Throat-Kick) to her throat (nodo)."

While based on the training I have put you through, and the Dragon Slayer blood coursing through your veins. You are kicking ass and stopping alien zombies. Nice work, it looks like you have knocked her out of service for a few, so let's get out of here before she recovers, because she has a future meeting with my other self in this year 2026. I know we are shaking the future up on a high level, based on what we have done so far by coming back to this year 2026.

Our hope is to rewrite the past, and change our future for the better, but when we can keep certain things somewhat the same. This might not be a bad idea, so Cleaning Witch can live for now, but now she knows what time it is, Time to Clean the Fucking Dojo!

TURN THE RADIO UP

Year 2026

Irish Warrior let's swing past your house, and get some more supplies, just in case we get held up somewhere, and need food and water, along with other possible on the go supplies. I know you have some stuff stocked up for just an occasion. Plus, I have a different idea or way to get the Hive Queen in our sights. Meaning we have been trying to find her, now it's time for this Hive Queen bitch to find us. When we get back to your house, we will go over the plan I have come up with.

Olivia, when we get back to Irish house, run a complete life/ health check on Sullivan, Sandra, Irish Warrior, and yourself. I'm especially interested to see Sullivan, Sandra and you return to your normal age, physically and mentally.

"You got Sir, I will start the full process now, and we should have results soon."

"I made good time back to my house; Clint I will get the bailout bag supplies for the road.

Ok, Burendo Shotokan Warriors, line up and get your goody bags. Here they are, when it comes to the best survival bag on the market with quality gear and supply, along with a most reasonable price. Nothing is more top shelf than the "All Hazards Tactical". This survival bag can get a person through tough days ahead and keep you in the fight for survival."

Absolutely Irish Warrior, you can't go wrong with this gear bag, it covers it all. You never know when this will come in handy. Looks like these All-Hazards Tactical bags are set up for 3 days of supplies. Enough food, water filtration/ purification, medical and shelter, along with other survival gear to keep us going. If memory serves me there are two types of bags, one is a rural kit, and another is an urban kit, depending on your needs and the environment you find yourself in. On a side e note, this business was started by a fellow Peace Officer and his wife, so he has a background of knowledge in survival, which just adds to the reliability, and credibility of this survival bag. Let's be honest, if we don't take care of business in the next couple of days. The human race is fucked on an alien-zombie shitstorm level anyways, but nothing is better than ALL HAZARDS TACTICAL when the Dead Adrenaline Alien-Zombie Apocalypse comes knocking, this bag will do the talking.

ALL HAZARDS TACTICAL

147

Olivia are the medical test completed on Sullivan, Sandra and you, along with the Irish Warrior.

"Perfect timing Sensei, the results have just come in, and it is remarkable in nature."

Spill the beans Olivia, humanity is waiting.

"Yes Sir, ok I will start with Irish Warrior, he is fit and sound, no signs of the blood infection. Also, his immune system is off the charts, meaning he won't catch any type of cold ever again in his lifetime. Plus, for some unknown reason, his body's reflexes have improved, which is a good thing to have in battle. Your blood has somehow made him stronger, faster, better than he was before. Also, only one visible side effect has been discovered when the Dragon Slayer blood is administered. It will change the color of the person's eye to a bright light blue shade, which gives that person night vision when needed. Meaning this person can turn it on like a flashlight or off. Crazy, but not a bad side effect, along with all the other benefits. Actually, from a medical standpoint, all of the side effects are beneficial, whether seen or unseen.

"See Clint, like I said before, Dragon Slayer blood powering through my veins."

Funny one Irish Warrior, yea you are improved like the 1973-1978, five season, Tv series, Six Million Dollar Man, starring Lee Majors. In your case, the cost is the price of a cheap ass syringe, and my priceless blood. Based on this, and the fact it doesn't take much to improve you, this would make you the Five Dollar & Fifteen Cent Man. Same wages we were making Irish, back when we started in law enforcement, I remember carrying a 686 Stainless steel,

Smith & Wesson on my hip, wondering if I should rethink my career choices. Times have changed, now I carry a ray gun and fight Zombie- Aliens. Crazy how the hammer of life falls and chips away, but at the same time moves forward to the future.

"Why am I friends with you Clint, I know why, because you have issues, but I like it. Plus, I bet your Dragon Slayer blood will be worth more than you would think in the future. Look how much it is worth to us right now; it is a cure on a massive level.

Good stuff Irish, I know, my blood might be the fountain of youth, or at least in some form or fashion a weapon against these savage DA(s). Sorry got sidetracked with the Irish Warrior cure, and the Bionic Man bullshitting, continue on with your findings Olivia.

"No problem, Sensei, I have learned over time being around you, to let you go. The brilliant thing is, blended in the busting of chops, nostalgia, movie magic, and tv memories are solid golden eggs of truth, and wisdom."

Irish did I mention Olivia is my top Burendo Shotokan Warrior student and is known for her insightfulness and observation skills.

"No, you didn't, but I see and hear what you are saying. HA!"

"OK, so I completed the test results on Sullivan, Sandra and myself as I stated earlier. The cure has worked, and our body's internal clock has reset. This means in approximately 10-15 minutes, Sandra, Sullivan, and I will return to our proper age, physically, and mentally. The painful trauma from the Cleaning Witch's bite and the blood injection of Sensei Clint's blood worked. The reverse age disease was in full effect, and the very beginning stage of the blood poisoning was introduced to our bodies. All of this medical trauma going down in DA town was just what the Dragon Slayer's blood needed, and it went to work and slayed the Alien Dragon. Now everyone might ask how is it that we will return to our normal age, mentally and physically, in such a quick way.

Simple, just like the human body takes longer to lose weight and get healthier, it takes a shorter time to gain weight and get unhealthy. In this case, the opposite is true, we will get healthier quicker than it took to get unhealthy, even though for us, we thought the reverse age disease was working at a very fast rate. I know this is strange medical science, but sometimes the cure is right there being carried around. Sensei had the cure and didn't even know it. Sorry Sensei, I am being long winded about this, but I have some other very important test results to report. This is a game changer for the human race."

No worries, continue with this information Olivia, and then I will unmask my plan to locate the Hive Queen.

Thanks, Sir, ok here are some fantastic test results that really matter for this battle against these alien animals. First, we were all injected with Sensei's Dragon Slayer blood, which now means we are stronger and improved in every way. Meaning, that our bodies can no longer get alien blood poisoning from a bite of these extraterrestrial cannibalistic savages. We can still get eaten alive or dead by these Dead Adrenaline aliens, but if they eat us, it will kill the alien host contained inside the human body. I also believe this can happen if the human carrier isn't too far gone, the human will survive, and recover because it had some of the Dragon Slayer blood transferred into their system, due to the dining habits of the DA. You understand what I'm saying! Sensei's blood is the cure to kill off these alien shits and save most of the population in the process.

Also, any of our blood now works the same way Sensei blood works to cure and kill aliens."

Holy Excalibur Dragon Slayer sandwich, this is one astonishing discovery Olivia. If I'm hearing what you are saying, this can save the future by way of a different direction or pathway.

"Exactly Sensei!"

"Exactly is correct, Olivia, Clint, Sandra and Sullivan, we need to send someone back to the future year of 2086, so their blood can be used to prevent, cure and kill some alien A-holes."

Spot on Irish Warrior! Now we must decide who will go back to the year 2086.

Yep, a choice must be made, obviously Irish Warrior, and I won't be going back, so it is down to Sandra, Sullivan or you Olivia. On a side note, I see that you guys have all returned to your normal age mentally and physically. Crazy shit, the change happens so very fast, no more children around, which is great outcome.

"I know Sensei, it is good to be back. It was a horrible place to be, my body didn't feel like my own, and my mind felt like it was slipping away every moment I attempted to remember. It was like when you drop something onto the floor, and attempt to find it, but you never do. I mean never ever find it again, even though you know it is somewhere down there. Then eventually you forget what you were looking for, and the painful memory loss continues over, and over again, until nothing is left."

Yeah, really terrible place to be Sandra, sorry this happened to you and Sullivan, but payback is on the food table now. The time to destroy these outer space assholes is on their doorstep now.

I will do it Sensei, let me go back, and I will bring the blood cure pumping through my veins to the year 2086.

Ok Sullivan, you will be the one that goes back to the year 2086. Hopefully you can start fighting these aliens in the future, and we will work on it in the past. Maybe battling it from both ends will annihilate their existence from the face of our earth.

Irish and Olivia will go over the medical protocol, and steps to administer the blood cure. Along with all the information needed to spread the word.

We might just do this thing, if the timing is right, and you make it back in one piece Sullivan. Think about it, if a DA bites someone, not only will they not get the DA blood poisoning, but the transfer of that person's blood will kill the alien entity inside the infected person's body, and as it was discovered, the human that was taken over, can survive. This only occurs if that human has been injected already with the Dragon Slayer Blood, which originated from my blood. On the flip side of this death-coin is trying to convince a person to let a Dead Adrenaline Zombie bite them without getting eaten alive. Meaning if a person has been bitten already, and they don't have the Dragon Slayer blood in them, they can be injected after and be saved. I guess what I am trying to describe in further detail is we need a large number of people to get the Dragon Slayer's blood and let the DA(s) bite them in hopes of curing the individual that has been taken as a host by the aliens.

Olivia and Irish Warrior, get Sullivan and Sandra up to speed on how this blood cure works. Both of them were too far gone with memory loss when we discovered this fantastic blood cure (Dragon Slayer blood).

"This won't take long Sensei; they are both quick learners in this area of survival."

Sounds good to me Olivia, once we send Sullivan off in the Time break pod, I will explain our next move to speed up finding Hive Queen.

"Hey Clint, both Sandra and Sullivan are all caught up on the Dragon Slayer blood miracle. Sullivan knows what he needs to do upon his return to the year 2086."

Ok Irish, good quick work explaining it.

You ready Sullivan, times a ticking, plus after you are launched, I need to leave Irish Warrior house, because my other self will be arriving sooner than later.

"OK Sensei Clint, if I don't ever see you again in this lifetime, it was an honor to be trained under your leadership. You have taken my fighting ability and respect for martial arts to another level. Thank you, Sir, and I will take care of the shit sandwich in the year 2086."

"Now you're talking my language Sullivan," Thank you right back, you stand tall, because you are everything a Burendo Shotokan Warrior should be. **GOD** is got your back, and your fighting skill will do the rest. You are carrying the cure of **Dragon Slayer** Blood, which is coursing through your veins, complete your mission.

Olivia get Sullivan ready for his return time travel.

"Ok Sensei, I broke out the Time travel pod setup. Sullivan is prepared to be launched; everyone stand back here it goes. Hopefully, the launch area in the year 2086 is in decent enough condition and has rebooted to take incoming visitors. If not, based on my calculations for the Time travel pod, Sullivan will return to the year 2086 but might end up outside the protective zone. If that happens, he will have to fight his way back to a safe area and make contact with officials to spread the word about the cure." "It's ok Olivia, let's do this."

"Take care Sullivan, hope to see you in the future soon."

(Sullivan vanishes as if he never existed in the year 2026, the future people of 2086 will be getting a visitor hopefully.)

OK, the deed is done, now here is the plan, and objective. We are going to the Beaver County Radio Station, once there we will gain entry, and hopefully get the airwaves up, and running. The power goes off and on as you know, due to alien interference, but that station has a generator I believe that can help with the broadcast. Also, we might get lucky, and the power just kicks back on. I want to send out a message to any person surviving in the terminal realm of Beaver County. We need to let them know there is a cure, and that our team is here to change the outcome of this invasion.

"Sensei, won't this message or alert get back to Hive Queen, and indicate our location, and objective."

Yes, that is exactly the purpose, Sandra, we are done looking for the Hive Queen, she will come to find us, just as she did before when I battled her at the One Strike Karate Dojo. I will tell you this, she will bring her DA minions with her in large numbers. Hive Queen doesn't like to lose and still wants me as a host human. As far as the Dragon Slayer blood cure, I bet she thinks this is a joke, and nothing can stop her. Time will tell the tale, t's gear up we're going to the radio station. Irish are you coming or staying here to wait for my other self to show up.

"You know what Clint, let's do this thing. I will be coming with you, I figure if we don't stop this invasion today, and now. The chances are basically over, so I guess the Clint from 2026 presently will have to figure things out without my help. Even though I am helping him / you, just in a different way."

Excellent Irish Warrior, I agree with that decision, even though we are changing the future, by action we are taking now, it's the right course of action. Plus, I'm a better version of myself now, hell I got Dragon Slayer blood.

"Yep, you are one Medieval Ninja Warrior."

Funny Irish, the Medieval Ninja Warrior saves the world. I think I will stick with "THE MAN CALLED CLINT" if that's alright.

"Ok, Clint, I get it, lol."

Time to move, we're heading to the Beaver County Radio station, the time has come for us to end this death game and save humankind. We will take two vehicles, Cool Blue 2086, fly ahead to the radio station. Cool Blue 2026 will ride with us.

(The Burendo Shotokan Warriors travel to their destination for a final battle, along the way, bloody carnage of roadkill is laying throughout the area of travel. Except it is dead human beings, lifeless on the ground. Some are just pieces of human flesh, and others are only half eaten carcasses. The invisible smell of death is watching with happiness. A gathering is occurring amongst the Dead Adrenaline savages, forces greater than their hunger for human flesh, and blood has summoned these evil entities

155

of hate to the meet with the Hive Queen at the Cracker /
Fracking plant, just has before, even though the future has
been altered, this gathering of the Dead Adrenaline
creatures is still occurring.)

There it is, the one and only top shelf Beaver County
Radio station, best in Beaver County. Great owners and
staff, excellent radio shows, news, weather reporting, and
sports. One stop radio station that simply has it all.

Beaver County Radio Station

"Sensei! You see the Dead DA lying in the parking lot to the far left side of the building."

I do Sandra, someone must have killed that roaming DA, not sure how that went down in DA town, but let's score one for the good guys, even though that DA corpse might have been a decent human being before the Dead Adrenaline apocalypse stricken the land of Beaver County. It looks like the DA took a spike to the top of the head, and whoever did this dispatching of this DA, got very lucky and hit the kill shot on the first attempt. Mr. Spike never stood a chance against this person. By the way, if you haven't figured it out by now everyone, I like to give nicknames out, especially to the DA(s) we encounter on this mission. Irish Warrior definitely knows this about me.

"I sure do know this, at least the nickname you gave me is a solid, cool nickname."

Yeah, I did have a couple of uncool ones that made no sense, so you're lucky. Ones like Irish Springy or Itchy Irish. Lol. Just joking really, the only nickname I ever had was Irish Warrior.

"Good one Clint. I have to say, I really, really don't know why I'm friends with you."

"Olivia run a postmortem scan to see how long Mr. Spike has been lying on the concrete in his checked-out state."

"Ok Sensei, the scan is being done as we speak. It looks like he has been in this state and location for about 48 hours. Also, Mr. Spike suffered a puncture to the top of the head from an unknown weapon or tool. A pipe or gun barrel shaped impact mark was left. Also, this indicates that this alien infection started even sooner than we suspected."

Spike

Interesting thought, I wonder if the person involved is still around or nearby because we're always looking for recruits in this battle against evil. On a lighter thought, the mention of 48 hrs., brings back memories of one of my favorite buddy cop movies, the 1982 American flick 48hrs, starring, Eddie Murphy and Nick Nolte. It really was a great team up on the big screen, plus you can't go wrong when you mix action and comedy in a perfect symphony of entertainment. On a musical note, the cool song, "The Boys are Back in Town" was featured in the soundtrack for the movie 48 hrs. The American rock group, "The Busboys" sang that song for the movie. Incidentally, this group also had another song, "Cleaning Up The Town" featured on the soundtrack for the 1984 movie Ghostbusters, starring Harold Ramis, Bill Murray, Dan Aykroyd, Ernie Hudson, and Sigourney Weaver to name a few. Anything with Sigourney in it is in my movie catalog.

 "Geez Sensei, you really got lost in the movie and music nostalgia, time to put on the brakes, we are trying to save the world."

This is true Sandra, but even in times like this, when the Boys and Girls come back to DA town, and they just so happen to be Burendo Shotokan Warriors.

One must find their place of peace and calmness to prepare for battle. My place on this day happens to be Movie and Music magic but make no mistake my focus goes beyond what you see or hear.

"Sorry Sensei, I know, it keeps you going."

There you go Sandra girl; you're catching on to my secret of life.

"Wow Clint, Sandra is a pretty confident lady, she decided to say what she is thinking."

Yep Irish, she is a woman of few words, but when she speaks you better believe it's for good reason. This is one of the reasons I picked her for the mission. Plus, it probably wasn't a good time to get lost in Music or Movie magic. Lol.

"You know my thoughts, Clint, you got issues, but that's why I am friends with you."

Ok, Irish Warrior and Burendo Warriors, let's move in and gain access to the building. Be ready, because you never know what will be found on the other side of these doors.

Irish, send both Cool Blues up to the front door, and I am sure between the both of them, the door lock can be opened.

"This will be child's play for them Clint, Blue 26 and 86, go unlock the door."

"Team, get ready, once the door is open, we will enter in a most tactical manner, and clear the facility."

(Both Cool Blues use magnetic hand movements on the outside of the door, Blue 26 is pulling away while touching the door lock with his android palm facing down, and Blue 86 is pushing forward into the door lock with his android palm. A Hikite (Pulling) and OSU(Pushing) technique of choice, the door lock releases with ease.)

Really nice Irish, the android brothers used some Magnetic hikite and Osu technique to open the door lock. Incidentally for wisdom purposes, "OSU" in the Japanese arts means to push, endure, to have patience mind, with perseverance, and determination. This is our compass to win the day. Let's enter the building now.

"Sensei! the building is clear and secure, except for the radio broadcasting room at the end of the hallway."

Ok, Sandra and Olivia, keep on the outskirts of this room. Irish and I will clear the room.

Irish let's kick the door open, enter and clear it just like old times back in the day when we used to bust Einstein criminals.

"You got it Clint, why don't you use one of your Burendo Shotokan front thrust kicks and knock this door in."

Yep, a maegeri-kekomi (front thrust kick) is just what is needed. Let's move!

(With unstoppable accuracy, power, and speed the door collapses like a paper castle. The Man Called Clint, and Irish Warrior enter the broadcasting room without hesitation, and total focus. While inside this room an unexpected person is located inside the room space. This individual is ready for battle, which brings to mind "Do not go gentle into that good night." (Written by Welsh Poet and writer Dylan Marlais Thomas.)

"Clint, do you see what I'm seeing standing before us in a very focused, I'm going to kick your ass stance."

I do Irish, it is none other than the one, and only broadcasting giant, Mr. Eddy Crow. The legend in broadcasting is here, and ready for battle.

Eddy, cool your jets, and to take a page from your radio play book, we are friends, and not Jag offs!

"What do you think Clint, Eddy is just looking at us with a very serious look of confidence."

I think he is about to say something Irish.

Eddy Crow

"You both are exactly right, I see that the Orwellian future has been unleashed, and the end of time has arrived. Except, it isn't just the government trying to control the narrative, an unknown Zombie-type takeover has arrived. Neighbors are too busy fighting for their lives, so no one will have the time to tell on one another. Also, with the power going off at the radio station, freedom of speech is being suppressed, along with independent thought."

You are so very correct Eddy, the Government is trying to control the narrative, and want the people of Beaver County, and the people of the world not to know the truth. As for the Zombie-type takeover, it is on a more out-of-this-world level. Aliens are here, they take many forms, humans are being infected by them, and they are using the human shell as a home, along with the earth. These Alien-Zombies love the taste of human flesh and blood, so they will try to eat you. Also, an alien entity that hasn't found a human home or needs a new one will try to break your will and take you over. This is the short version of current events Eddy. Similar to George Orwell, Nineteen Eighty-Four of an Orwellian future you were mentioning, but different in many ways.

"Interesting, so we got a little bit of Soylent Green action going on out there, humans eating humans, but in a very different way than the movie."

Good for you Eddy, you must be a poet, and movie fan. By the way, yea the Government is trying to cover up humans eating humans, but in a different way than the 1973 ecological dystopian thriller movie Soylent Green as you mentioned. Yep, you can't go wrong with any Charlton Heston movie. I have to say, things are turning into more of the 1971 post-apocalyptic action flick Omega Man, which also starred Charlton Heston. Never really thought about it, but maybe Mr. Heston knew something we didn't, even back then. Lol.

"What is your name and your friend's, who is next to you."

My name is Clint, and this guy beside me is Irish Warrior.

"Don't let Clint fool you Eddy, he is known by the world as The Man Called Clint."

"Irish Warrior, I figured as much, based on this short dialogue we have had in these passing moments. You must be one of his best friends, because I see you got his back. The name Irish Warrior definitely suits you."

"Clint you would make for a great guest on my Beaver County Radio show, we could talk about movies, poetry, and I'm sure you would have written a book by then."

Funny you mentioned a book Eddy, because I have written a journal about the Dead Adrenaline occurring in Beaver County and may write a second one based on what has been occurring in the year 2026, this second time around. You will definitely be in that second book. Lol.

"OK Clint two questions, what is Dead Adrenaline, and what do you mean your second time in the year 2026."

Yeah, Eddy, there is a lot to cover in a short time, but I will say this. The name Dead Adrenaline or DA was given to these alien zombies, which kind of sums up what these things could be. Maybe they are dead or maybe they're alive. If you encounter one of these DAs, you will understand this name totally.

"I do Clint, in fact, I encountered one of them outside in the parking lot when I was coming into work. You see, I pulled into the Beaver County radio parking lot this morning and noticed no one had arrived yet. I thought this was very odd, so I parked my vehicle and went over to the side door to enter the radio station, and that's where it happened. I felt a presence moving towards me, so I looked to my left, and there it was just standing about 10 feet away from me. I thought to myself, who in the hell is this **Jag-Off** just standing there and glaring? A closer look and it was apparent that this human being wasn't human anymore. It had blood-red eyes, and its body looked to be deteriorating with every breath and movement it took. Anyway, I moved as fast as I could and attempted to make a run for my vehicle. This thing was hungry, and it started to pick up speed towards me. At that point, I had two choices to pick from, either live or die. I decided to live obviously, so within that moment of decision-making, I fought and managed to spike that DA right on top of its cranium. Dropped him like a bad radio show, right onto the concrete parking lot,

I believe the body is still lying outside as we speak. You see, I carry a handgun with me for self-protection, even though I know it's illegal, and the United States Controlled Military (USCM), along with the Government, which doesn't allow it. I never got rid of it or gave it up, obviously getting ammunition has become an issue, but I still have a supply that I stockpiled for rainy day."

"Yeah, sometimes tough choices have to be made when stupid laws are implemented that only really mess with the law-abiding citizens. Anyway, the funny thing was I pulled out my handgun and went to shoot this crazy, red-eyed savage, and the gun wouldn't fire. No malfunction was discovered in the seconds that I had; it just wouldn't fire. At that moment, I reacted and completed a downward hit to the top of this DA's skull. I hit him with the barrel of the gun and the attack was over within seconds. After I took out this jag-off Alien-Zombie human, I went back to my vehicle, but it wouldn't start, so I made it back to the radio station and locked myself in. I figured someone would show up eventually, and with my access to radio broadcasting, I could let the public know, and maybe the People Peace Protectors (PPP) would show up. Unfortunately, I haven't been able to use the radio, because the power doesn't stay on long enough or at all, so no radio announcement has been able to be aired."

Well, I work for the PPP, and I can tell you with certainty this law enforcement agency won't be stopping by because this Dead Adrenaline invasion and infection has a rear naked choke (Hadaka Jime) on Beaver County. Also, now we know who took out the DA, I named Mr. Spike, due to your handy work. Eddy, you are going to need caught up on what has actually happened in Beaver County.

You see these blue colored androids; their names are Cool Blue 26 and Cool Blue 86. They will get you hooked up with video and audio about this tragic takeover of Beaver County.

"This is really Cool Clint."

I know Eddy, those bots are badass.

(Eddy Crow was updated on the current events destroying Beaver County, and the state of human species. The information given to Eddy was absorbed like a radio talk show host preparing for a show.)

"Well now that I'm caught up on what is going down in DA town and got to meet the rest of your team Clint, I guess you needed to make an announcement over the radio airwaves, and that's why you broke into the radio station."

This is true Eddy, and this announcement needs to be made for several reasons. The first reason is to warn the public about these zombie humans, and how to kill them. Also, a cure has been discovered, so they need to take shelter and avoid the outside areas. Lastly, the elimination of these alien invaders is in the works, but it will be a major undertaking.

Imminent Threat

Year 2026

One other thing, which is a shot to the dark side of the moon. I want to challenge the Hive Queen leader to show up outside of this radio station, and battle my Burendo Shotokan Burendo Warriors and I. The Hive Queen team, against my team, good versus evil. You see the Hive Queen is overconfident and believes with every breath of her alien being, no one can stop her. I believe she is out there waiting in the blood shadows for a personal invitation because she and I have unfinished business.

"Listen Clint, I know what you're thinking, and I will do the announcement. It's what I do for a living, tell people stuff, and talk about issues and concerns. Plus, this alien invasion is a top story that needs to be talked about, and I have to say, my grandma would want the full story told."

I expected nothing-less from the Master of the radio show stage, this is your Martial Art of choice Eddy.

"Yeah, Clint, this radio forum is my place of calmness, nostalgia and focus. Plus, I do love to talk and listen to what's going on locally and around the world. I do have a question, how are we going to get the power up and running again at the Beaver County Radio station, long enough to get this alert message out."

Leave this up to Irish Warrior, who is technology genius of sorts, he is working on getting the system back in running form with the help of two android friends, Cool Blue 2026 and Cool Blue 2086. They have a power source that these aliens haven't figured out how to shut off. Just another badass thing we got going on in our fight against these A-hole aliens.

"Clint, did I mention those Androids are really cool."

You did Eddy, and they are the best bots in the business of fighting aliens. Lol.

Ok, Olivia, and Sandra, once the announcement is made, be ready for the riot of pure evil to show up in large numbers. You see, Hive Queen loves to make a grand entrance, just another one of her flaws, just be ready for violence on a whole new level.

Irish how is it going with the power issue.

"Give me two more seconds and we will be back on the air. OK, the power is on, and now it's up to Eddy to do the rest. Anyways, everyone, an unexpected thing occurred, due to the power source being generated from my Cool Blue team bots, the broadcast will not only air in Beaver County, PA, but the entire United States will hear this broadcast. Given that, this will impact the present and the future of the human race."

Great work Irish and Cool Blue 26 and 86. It is time to remove the veil of lies and cover-up that our government and leaders have been projecting to the citizens of the United States.

Eddy, it's all you buddy, time for some radio magic to hit the airwaves, and let the words fly.

"I hear what you are saying Clint, and I'm ready to "Turn the Radio up" and unleash my idiosyncrasy way of speaking to the people. When this broadcast is completed the human race and the alien race will know the battle line has been drawn in the concrete sand of Beaver County, PA."

It's your show now Eddy, let your masterful words, hit the airwaves like a Mawashi-Geri (Roundhouse-Kick) to the jaw of these Aliens.

"OK, we are on the air now! Good evening radio listeners this is Eddy Crow, and what I am about to say is going to be shocking on a level that you may never hear again. This is an imminent threat alert! I will cut to the fact-based information, so the public can hopefully save themselves. As I speak, we are being invaded by alien beings from another world, they have surfaced on our planet and are taking over human minds and bodies, which turns a human being into an alien zombie-like creature. They have been given the name Dead Adrenaline, and these cabalistic humanoids will eat you for dinner. They love the taste of human flesh and blood. If their eyes are solid red that means they are very hungry and aggressive. If their eyes are blue mixed with red, this means they have eaten, but they will still try to attack you. If you are bitten, a form of alien blood infection poisoning will eventually take your life, so be aware not to get bitten. In a positive direction, they can be killed, you must keep striking, kicking, or using any weapon or object you can find, and get lucky enough to land a kill shot. These Dead Adrenaline Zombies have weak spots on their bodies. If you find this weak area, they can be killed. I know a human life is involved, but they are no longer human at that point, even though they might be dead, or they might be alive you must fight back if you want to survive. Also, if you are still listening out there, don't give in, have fortitude and the strength to avoid giving up.

These alien entities will seize that moment of weakness and take over your mind and body. If this happens, you will become a Dead Adrenaline soldier of evil.

169

A team from the future, which is being guided by a leader named "The Man Called Clint" has come from the future year of 2086. They are working on a definite way to stop these alien A-holes, which are being led by an evil creature called the "Hive Queen." A cure has been found but getting it out to the public is still a work in progress, so take shelter, and stay away from crowded areas.

Lastly, this message is for the Hive Queen bitch! The Man called Clint is waiting for you at the Beaver County Radio Station, and he believes you are afraid and won't accept his challenge, so here is what I'm saying loud and crystal clear, you JAG-OFF alien leader! The Man called Clint, knows you can't beat him or the human race. You see, he knows you are weak and a pathetic alien race that hides in the blood shadows preying on the weak. If you are listening, come find him, but we all know you won't, because you are outmatched, and deep down in your black blood-soaked heart you know this. This is Eddy Crow signing off, please stay safe everyone, and remember to watch out for those Alien-Zombie jag-offs."

Holy triple shit sandwich Eddy, that was fantastic, and man you definitely pissed off the Hive Queen.

"Yeah, Clint that was my intention."

(Within the distance, a piercing, shrieking scream of hatefulness echoes repeatedly from outside with enough power and force that a wave of this hideous sound surrounds everyone inside the building. Pain and suffering is coming, and the challenge has been accepted.)

"Shit Clint, Hive Queen is really furious, and she is on her way."

Yep Irish Warrior, she accepted my challenge given out by Eddy, now it's time to prove that we aren't all show and no-go.

"No doubt about it, Clint, she is one nasty alien. Sorry, I might have overdone the invite."

It's all good Eddy, you set the wheels in motion with your gut-punch announcement, and now I will end this Bull shit storm today. Plus, now the entire United States knows what's going on in DA town if they choose to accept the truth.

"Clint, I was thinking about something that might be possibly linked to this alien invasion. I remember a police report from many years ago, long before this Dead Adrenaline apocalypse rolled into town. This incident involved two detectives who were working on a case involving mysterious unexplained murders in Pittsburgh PA. There was a brief report given out that bodies were showing up dead throughout the City of Pittsburgh. Some reports suggested that these murders were so violent that a human-like Zombie was doing the killings. I actually can't remember if they ever solved these crimes, but wow, it does make you think, what if there was more to this story."

City Of Pittsburgh

You know what Eddy, I remember this case that
happened in the City of Pittsburgh, in fact, believe it or not,
I knew the detectives that investigated these murders,
Detective Katsutoshi Shiokawa and Detective Jones. You
see, Shiokawa was from Japan, and he was really good
friends with David Jones, who lived in the United States.
Both of these Detectives were experts in the field of crime
solving and were sought after for difficult investigations that
involved supernatural and unusual circumstances.

I know they have worked on investigations in the past, but
they were the ones involved in these bizarre Zombie-like
murders. You see when I say, I knew these guys, it's
because they were both martial art students of mine, back
when I was teaching at One Strike Karate, long before this
Dead Adrenaline shitstorm landed in Beaver County, PA. If
memory serves me, at that time they were investigating a
"Murder At Witches' Hollow" which was very supernatural
and mysterious in itself. Anyways, they are great guys with
solid fortitude and had the will to overcome. This

conversation does make me think, what if that Zombie-like human was possibly involved in that investigation Shiokawa and Jones were trying to solve? It wasn't just a human or just a zombie, but an alien from another planet. Maybe a test subject alien, sent to see if planet Earth would be a conducive environment for their species, along with a human body being taken as a host.

"You mean a decider, just to test the food, shelter, and population."

Yeah Eddy, a decider that was sent long before this Dead Adrenaline invasion hit Beaver County, PA.

"Well, they must have liked the alien decider's review, because Earth definitely made the list of suitable planets with a habitat that blended well for these aliens somewhat."

This is true Irish Warrior, but now it is time to kick these alien creatures off our planet.

"Ok. Clint, I'm going to send out some surveillance. Cool Blue 2086, go fly around the outside parking lot area of the building, and send back some video footage when the first signs of the DA(s) show up."

Good idea Irish. Olivia and Sandra get your weapons of choice ready because the fight will be on our doorstep soon.

"Shit! Some video live footage just came back from Cool Blue 2086, and it looks like the DA(s) are showing up in large numbers. No sign of Hive Queen, as of yet. Clint, I will have Cool Blue 2026 show the live footage sent from Cool Blue 2086.",

They have Arrived!

Good idea Irish, this will show everyone what we're dealing with in DA town. Come take a look everyone, into death's eyes.

"Clint, I just got some-more footage, and this doesn't look promising. The Dead Adrenaline apocalypse has arrived in full force, and these DA(s) look to be very aggressive and hungry.

Ok Irish, put that footage up to look at, let's see what we're going to be dealing with this time around.

"You got it Clint, Cool Blue 2026 go ahead and project this footage on the radio station wall. I bet Cool Blue 2086 could put out a hologram projection image, but Cool Blue 2026 is still old school."

"Oh, this is dreadful for us Sensei, along with the video footage sent back to us from Cool Blue 2086. A scan was done on these DA(s), and their adrenaline test is off the charts. Meaning they have no flight in their system, just fight!"

Put this in your memory banks people, because Olivia's data scan on these DA(s) is more accurate than a kill shot placed by a Burendo Warrior. Take a look at what we will be battling, it might be dead, or it might be alive, but it is present and very hungry. The berserk nature of these DA(s) seems different from the ones I have dealt with before. Even though they look to be unhinged and frantically waiting to release their terror on us, along with the rest of the human race, they are thinking and planning out what their next moves will be. This makes them a more dangerous advisory because any human or alien life form is more of a threat when they are blending their mind and body in a large-scale death match.

Pain

Suffering

DEAD ADRENALINE

Very strange, and unexpected, these DA soldiers are facing away from the Beaver County Radio station building. They must have been some of the first humans to get infected because they appear to be more deteriorated than the first groups that showed up, but their actions can mean only one thing, they are awaiting their Queen. Yep, Hive Queen is coming, and it doesn't care if we know this. Talk about telegraphing your technique in this Kumite (Free Fight) battle. In this case, Hive Queeny is doing this intentionally to show her dominance. This is a very creepy, and shocking sight to behold. Also, it indicates that Hive Queen appears to have got her cannibalistic DA(s) in working order.

"Clint, the number of DA(s) that have shown up is astronomical. This is going to be an undertaking on a massive level. I will fight to the death but are you seeing what I'm seeing."

I do Irish, it appears that Hive Queen is throwing all of her DA soldiers into the mix. She is here to win and will not accept defeat. We need to thin the horde of DA(s), which will be a high-level undertaking. If they bite us, they could die from the Dragon Slayer blood exchange, but we could bleed out in the process or get eaten alive. We need to find a way to get this Dragon Slayer blood into their system, which could save some of the humans that have been changed into DAs.

"Sensei, there is a way to get this Dragon Slayer blood into the DA(s) system, but it is drastic and very wrong on so many levels."

Let's hear it Olivia, and don't candy coat any of it.

"OK Sensei, unfortunately, with the resources here and now in this year of 2026, we lack medical and scientific technology from the future year of 2086, so there's only one way of doing this blood transfer. You see, we can't just take blood from one of us and inject it into a DA. This will only work from human to human, but when it is an alien entity inside a human shell, the process has to be different. If we had the resources, the process of injecting DA(s) could be accomplished. Hopefully Sullivan and the Medical minds in the year 2086 are doing this as we speak, but for us the situation is different. The only way we can spread the Dragon Slayer blood is to have someone become a sacrifice, meaning they need to have the Dragon Slayer blood in their bloodstream as all of us do, so what I'm saying Sensei and everyone, this person will have to run out into the horde of DA zombies and become their meal. Once they are consumed, some blood transfer will take place that will kill the alien entity, and possibly save the human host if they aren't too far gone mentally or physically. If the human does survive and returns to the land of the living.

These humans will then become the DA(s) next victim, and the cycle will repeat with Dragon Slayer Blood transfer, which will eventually, and ultimately thin the horde of the walking dead adrenaline."

"This could eliminate these DA(s) totally over time, or at least, help dramatically. I know that the human beings that are released from their captivity of the alien entity will be getting a raw deal, when they come back to the land of the living, just to be facing death by getting ingested by the DA(s). This is wrong on so many levels, but they could survive, and it gives them some chance, instead of no chance. Sensei, and fellow fighters this is what it has come down to. In order to survive, we must sacrifice other humans, but this is the world we are living in everyone."

This is so true Olivia, now you are starting to sound like me, but this choice needs to be made because we have called out the Dogs of War, and the only way to fight this Demon Dog is to become like that dog.

"I will do it, Clint!"

Eddy! What are saying.

"Inject me with the Dragon Slayer Blood and I will start this chain of mayhem events."

Eddy, you know what you are embarking on, and volunteering to do, listen there's no way back from this. You will be suffering on a level never before felt, and you won't return from this.

"Clint, I know what the score is in this game, and we are losing. It's time for a touchdown, and I will make that play. You guys need to finish the game with your weapons of choice. Plus, my grandma always said, "be part of a winning solution, and not losing outcome."

Ok, Eddy.

Olivia, prepare the blood injection and take it directly from me, Eddy is about to get some Dragon Slayer Blood from the origin source.

"Ok Sir, I will get started."

"Clint, before we do this, I have a final request."

Yeah, what is it, Eddy?

"A last meal would be nice."

Ok, but I'm not sure what we could do about this. We do have some food supply from our "All Hazard Tactical" gear bag.

"I'm sure that would be good, but no Clint, I got something that will fit the bill."

What would that be Eddy?

"Pop Tarts, why not on this last meal type of day. I was a pop tart kid, you see I would sleep in longer before getting up for school, because I could eat a pop tart for breakfast on my way to school, if you believe what I'm saying."

Pop Tarts are really tasty stuff, but where are we going to get a box?

"Oh Clint, I got a supply here at the radio station, and my favorite flavor is brown sugar with frosting. Here everyone grab a pop tart."

Funny Eddy, Brown sugar with frosting is my favorite flavor too.

"Cool Blue 2026, hook up the toaster to your power source, we will heat up some Pop Tarts."

Great idea Irish Warrior. Grab a Pop Tart everyone, courtesy of Eddy.

"Wow Sensei this is really tasty, I never had a Pop Tart before."

Yeah Sensei, I love it, really yummy.

I know Sandra and Olivia; glad you like the taste because this might be a last meal for all of us.

"Clint, we need to pick up our pace, because Hive Queen just showed up, and looks pissed."

Pissed Off Hive Queen

Yep, not a happy smile coming from the Hive Queen this time. She is ready for battle, poor Kris must be really suffering right now, because that sick alien leader has taken her over already. Really sad to see Kris again in this state of punishment.

Yeah, you probably don't know this Eddy, but when I mention the name Kris, she was a soldier from this time who showed up and was taken over by Hive Queen.

The interesting and unusual thing everyone, Kris was taken over by the Hive Queen on the fourth day of my journey, the first go around in 2026, and not on the second day, which is now.

This means one thing without a blood shadow of a doubt, we have changed events of the future in this year 2026 already. You see, all of us being here battling DA(s) in a different moment, which never happened originally has changed the chain of future events. I bet the United States Controlled Military (USCM), and the leader of the United States started to panic that the truth would get out, so they sent in the USCM soldiers in sooner to possibly stop the bleed.

Wow! What a crazy shit sandwich this turned out to be. Nevertheless, Hive Queen is here and prepared to destroy us and the entire future of humankind.

It is time, Eddy.

Olivia, take some of my Dragon Slayer blood and give it to Eddy.

"Ok Sensei, here we go."

Eddy the deed is done, now it's up to you. God is waiting for you, I'm sure.

"Eddy the only visible side effect this blood injection will give you is bright light blue eyes."

"Olivia, thanks for the info. Yeah, it's been really nice to talk to you Clint, and everyone on your team, open up the door let's get this over with."

Alright everyone, things are about to get very treacherous, and we will have to make sacrifices that may go against our believe system of what is right or wrong. These choices will have to be made no matter the cost.

183

The survival of the human race is all that matters, so we must stay strong like a Yosai (Fortress), and win this war on this day, in this year of 2026. Our actions on this day will change the future of the planet earth, so fight with every breath of life you have in your body, be relentless, and battle within the code of the Burendo Shotokan Warrior. Now what time is it everyone!

(With a loud voice of total determination, Olivia, Sandra, and even the Irish Warrior, say the words to set the battle in motion. It's **Time to Clean The Fucking Dojo!!!**, Eddy Crow looks on with a slight smile of agreement, and with an understanding of what is about to go down in DA town, he bolts out the front door and makes a run towards the horde of DA(s). Eddy starts to fight off the crowd of Dead Adrenaline walking, knowing the outcome will be death, The DA(s) viciously attack and bite Eddy as he moves his body towards the center of the nightmare. At that moment, he stops fighting back, and the cannibalistic savages close-in as he stands ready for his final song in his life. Eddy quickly disappears into the mob of DA(s), and just like warriors of the past that were sacrificed by being thrown off a cliff, no scream is heard as Eddy falls to his death.

(A silent fall by a brave warrior, willing to sacrifice himself to save the human race and planet earth. The Man Called Clint, Irish Warrior, and the Burendo Shotokan Warriors watch the carnage unfold, and know in their hearts a very honorably, true warrior gave his life for the cause.)

The Last Moments of Eddy Crow

Eddy's Last Breath

The Arrival of the King.

"Sensei! Some of the DA(s) are falling apart and appear to be losing their flesh from their bodies. All that is left is a skeleton that is collapsing to the ground. Also, it looks like some human hosts are changing back to their total human state but are getting devoured quickly by DA(s) after the change. The cycle is continuing, and the Dead Adrenaline numbers are thinning considerably, unfortunately in such a tragic way no humans are surviving from the DA onslaught."

Well, Olivia, at least it is working somewhat in the way we thought it would, but it is obvious that a small number of humans are returning back from the DA walking dead. Based on this, eventually, there won't be any more humans with the Dragon Slayer blood in them that will spread the cure, which can release a human from their alien prison. Sadly, the majority of humans don't change back and just melt away, along with the DA entity inside them. Similar to a kill-shot, which kills the DA, and the human host. What did we expect, this is DA town, and pain and suffering are always on the menu.

"Look, Clint, Hive Queen doesn't like what is going down, in fact, she looks puzzled and worried about the loss of such a great number of her DA front-line soldiers. Hive Queen just gave some kind of command that directed her other DA(s) to take out the rest of the humans that have changed back, they are just crushing their skulls in, minus feeding on the poor human souls. Looks like they made quick work of it, and now are reassembling by the Hive Queen."

Yep Irish, these alien savage DA(s) are thinking, and now they know that if they bite us, they will not survive when the Dragon Slayer blood enters their system. Also, we are no longer a viable host to take over. This is a real problem for these alien a-holes, so they need to end us and stop this from happening. Luckily, we did send Sullivan to the future, who also is a carrier of this bloodline cure. Maybe he and top medical minds of the future can figure out a better way that saves more humans.

"Sensei! A man is trying to get into the front doors of the radio station. He must have been able to break away from the DA crowd after he changed back and survived the trip to the land of the living."

Ok, Sandra, let's open the doors quickly and let him in before any DA(s) follow.

"Shit! This guy is a mess, he just ran in, and curled up in the corner of the hallway."

Let him be, he most likely won't be battling today anymore Sandra.

Olivia, run a health scan on him.

"You got it Sensei, it looks like he is totally DA infection free, but his mental and physical well being is a whole other issue."

Well, at least we know the Dragon Slayer Blood works, and can change a human back in some cases, but it looks like the rest of the walk back to being a human again is up to the individual.

"I will give him something to take the edge off his frightened state, this won't make him sleepy, but will help reboot his mind."

You're the Doctor Olivia girl, so do what you need to do. Thanks.

Ok, Irish what's the score, and what is the intelligence being sent back from Cool Blue 2086, to Cool Blue 2026. I know we could be just watching unfold on our optic lens, but like you have told me in private that we are too close to these alien shit storm, and Hive Queens power, which could shut down Cool Blue if too much technology is being used.

"Well Clint, the read out from both Cool Blues is the same, Hive Queen is becoming very agitated on a tremendous level. Also, she almost seems to be worried in a weird alien way and there's one other thing that isn't great news for us.

Something or someone is coming, and the slight readouts the Cool Blue Brothers were able to latch onto are saying this. A powerful type of reckoning is coming to planet earth. What is coming is of an unknown origin, but it has entered the earth's atmosphere and has plotted a course to our location. This powerhouse of energy is huge, and pure evil is traveling with it."

"Yep, Hive Queen must be waiting for it also, along with her DA soldiers, because they aren't moving towards the building to attack Sir. They have actually moved further from us."

Yeah, Sandra, something is coming, and whatever it could be worries the Hive Queen to the point she is waiting for its arrival.

"Clint, the Cool Blues just informed me that there is another life force heading towards our location, readouts indicate that it is two life forms, No other info could be identified, but it just appeared out of nowhere and should be here within 5 minutes, according to the speed of it, which is traveling at least 200 miles per hour. "

This is very unusual Irish, I feel a sense of calmness, nostalgia, and peace right now. Almost as if I'm somehow connected with what is about to arrive on our doorstep in the next few minutes.

"Well let's hope this is a good thing. Clint, because these life forms have just arrived."

Come on Irish, let's step outside for a moment because I believe this is a very good thing.

"Holy Shit, are you seeing what I'm seeing Clint?"

I do Irish, a badass Dragon, and the Silver Samurai flying in from the dark sky above, we have met before, minus the Dragon. No time to explain in detail, but she saved me from definite death. Yeah, I gave her the name Silver Samurai, because she battles like a Samurai, but wears traditional- style silver-coated armor with a medieval look.

Plus, that's a cool ass name that fits her. Yep, this warrior has just landed and has step down from the Dragon.

The Silver Samurai and Her Dragon!

"The Hive Queen and DA soldiers appeared to be a little shocked and confused because they had moved back even further from the Radio Station building. They must be assessing the situation in creepy fashion. I will have Cool Blue 2026 and 2086 keep a watch on Hive Queen, and her DA horde, if things change, we will know."

This is so true Irish Warrior. Hive Queen must be sizing up the battle attack situation. At least this will give us a little time to speak with the Silver Samurai and see what she is doing in DA town. I already know and feel a great force of pure goodness coming from her. I'm not sure how this can be, but maybe it's one of my newfound powers I got along with others, such as Dragon Slayer Blood. Ok, the Silver Samurai is walking up closer to us, let's hear what she has to say.

"Hi, Dad! It's me your daughter Chloe. I have come from the past, present and future for this moment in time. You see, I have prepared myself mentally and physically for this very time on Earth to battle these alien forces, alongside my dad, along with his Burendo Shotokan Warriors, and you Irish Warrior."

"Oh, hi Chloe."

"Hi Irish."

Chloe, I knew there was something that connected me to you. I felt the presence of that back when you saved me from that onslaught of DA(s) at the Daughtery Fire Hall grave lot. Chloe how's my girl doing, you were only 17 yrs. old the last time I saw you, now you must be in your twenties.

"Yeah Dad, I'm 23 yrs. old now, and have been on a very long adventure involving time travel, fight preparation, and a Dragons, but I will say this. I have trained many places throughout time, and I do have the Dragon Slayer Blood pumping through my veins. I have gained past, present, and future knowledge throughout our universe. Time-traveling ability has made advancing strides, which would amaze everyone here. I'm a product of this, you see, Sullivan did make it back to the year 2086, and he had a sample of the Dragon Slayer blood, which was taken from you in the year 2026. Along with that Sullivan himself was a carrier of a form of the Dragon Slayer blood, which he had been injected with to save his life when he was in the year 2026 with you guys. Anyways, the future did work on a possible cure, by, by administering the Dragon Slayer blood, but they only used blood from Sullivan and held on to the Pure Dragon Slayer Blood sample. It did help slow down the DA attacks and keep more people alive, but the Alien Hive Queen readapted and is still recalibrating her attack method, probably as we speak.

Anyways, through trial and error, it was discovered that once the dragon slayer blood was injected into a person, for example like Sullivan, and others the blood was watered down by the genetic qualities of that person, but still was powerful enough to destroy the majority of DA(s) that attacked. If you can wrap your brain around the whole time-travel thing, and the battle that continues in the year 2086, it was discovered that the only way the alien invasion could be stopped was to get a direct bloodline from the origin carrier of the Dragon Slayer Blood. Being that you're my father, the best person for this would be me, so they located me in the year 2086 at the old age of 78. Guess what Dad, Austin Maximillian found me, and yes, the Dragon Slayer blood from Sullivan brought him back to being human again. In fact, he was the first human subject to survive in the year 2086, and not be totally messed up from becoming a DA. OK, so when I was found, I embraced the opportunity to save humanity, and my dad "The Man Called Clint." For whatever so reason, when they gave me the full amount of blood sample of Dragon Slayer Blood taken directly from you, my body regenerated back to the ideal age of 23 yrs. old. I gained strength, and endurance on a level never seen before. Based, on this I needed to take my fighting skills even further than what I already knew from your teachings, so they sent me back to the year 2025, one year before the DA apocalypse occurred, and I started to enhance my training with Master G.

The future medical doctors, scientists, and government leaders felt that this would give me the best chance of success. During my time with Master G, I could only stay for a short time in that past year and return again. I had to repeat this type of time traveling numerous times until my body adapted to that year in time. You see Dad, everyone involved in this science project thought I wasn't affected by the reverse age disease because my past self was living in that year already. Just like I'm sure you believe this is part of the reason why you weren't cursed with the reverse age disease, along with your Dragon Slayer blood that crossed over into your body's bloodstream, from your first battle to the death with Hive Queen. We were all wrong, it doesn't matter if we exist in the year, we time travel to already. I have been to many different years in time, some of which I haven't even been born yet. You see, it was discovered that the Dragon Slayer blood is the secret, which you are the origin, which made the difference. Plus, I have Dragon Slayer blood in my system, which is of a pure bloodline. From Father to Daughter, which enhances all of my human abilities to a pure adrenaline level, which is off the charts.

Eventually, my body and mind adapted to whatever year I happened to time travel to, and ultimately, I felt like I had always been present in that year if that makes any type of time travel sense. Another interesting fact that was a beneficial side affect for both of us, is we can exist at the same time as our original version that are here in 2026. Coexisting can occur, because genetically we have changed, so we aren't exactly the same anymore. We are different, but the same. I will say this dad, I continued with my training after I left Master G. Also, I picked up Dragon along the way, his name is YOSAI, which means fortress. Yeah, Dad, this whole planet takeover invasion is not going well for the human race, and I feel a sense of another massive evil coming to us very shortly, and it will not be good. It must be a real malevolent evil in nature because now my sword has turned into Excalibur, and when I say Excalibur, I mean the actual real, authentic sword given to me from the Lady of the Lake, if you are up on your King Arthur knowledge, which I know you are dad. You see, Excalibur can only be wielded in the hands of a true King, and by the way this is a real sword, and not just a mythological artifact."

"What I'm saying is, I'm a Woman king in another time in history. No time to explain now, but I can bring the Excalibur from that era here when needed, otherwise, the Excalibur is safely secured in the magical stone mentioned in Arthurian legend, until called upon by yours truly. Yep, this is a lot to take in Dad, but I have trained and fought on the medieval battlefields with King Arthur, and the Knights of the Round Table, which has only improved my fighting skills. I have been trained in supernatural magical sorcery by Merlin Ambrosius, which was one hell of experience to say the least. Ok, sorry I'm all over the page, but I do have so much to tell you dad about my adventures, and the reason for them."

Silver Samurai.

Dragon named Yosai (Fortress)

Master G.

Really incredible, unbelievable stuff you are telling me. Great to see you Chloe, and obviously we are busy saving the world, so when we conquer this monster mayhem war. I most definitely would love to hear about your adventures, and how you came to be the Silver Samurai. Anyways, come on over here kid, and give your dad a hug. Well, I guess your not a kid anymore, you're the Silver Samurai. I was going to say, I got dragon slayer blood, and you got a dragon, but you have both. LOL.

"I do Dad, along with many other fantastic, and beneficial abilities. If you haven't caught it yet, my silver armor changes its look, based on the threat, or environment it encounters. Crazy as it sounds, my battle armor involuntarily controls what style, or type of armor I might need in battle. Also, this armor is extremely lightweight, unlike the typical ancient armor of the past. The same sort of thing happens with my weapon of choice, which is my sword. At first, in my many time travel adventures, my sword would change or modify, based on what I needed for a fight around me. Over time, my sword blade maintained a particular style more or less, only settle changes would

197

occur. Almost as if my mind and body knew, and the sword knew this worked best for me in the weapon-wielding department. Now this being said, I can command my sword to change its shape or style, if I so wish. Kinda like when I showed up the first time you saw me, wielding the *Haja-no-Ontachi (Great-Evil-Crushing Blade)*. On another cool note, this supernatural power occurs with my dragon Yosai to.

Meaning his dragon scales, and spikes on his head change, based on the threat, and environment we fly into. These powerful abilities almost act like they are alive in a way, how this came to be is a very fascinating, and unbelievable tale, which we don't have time to hear about, due to all this death on our doorstep. Dad, I have so many things, I would love to tell you about, but the final battle is near."

This stuff you're talking about is really cool, and I know Irish Warrior would love to talk about the technology behind it.

"I will say this Dad, these powers are mystical in nature, and not technology-driven."

Sounds like it, but I need to ask something quickly, how is Mom and Luke doing?

"Mom and Luke are in a very good place. Both my brother Luke and Mom miss you immensely. Mom (Kim) never gave up hope, and her love for you is unshakable, she told me this one thing that has kept me going to find you. She looked at me with total confidence and said these words, "I will see your dad again in this life or the next and I will be waiting for his return."

(For the first time in a long time, the Man Called Clint couldn't separate himself from the sadness, and pain of wanting to see his wife (Kim), and son Luke. At that moment, Clint knew this medieval battlefield was where death and life meet for the final act. If he and his team, along with the Silver Samurai, and her Dragon don't win on this day, at this moment in time. Human evolution is damned, and earthlings will never walk the Earth as a human ever again. At this very moment, The Man Called Clint felt like a void Somewhere in Time, kind of like the 1980 movie *Somewhere in Time,* starring Christopher Reeve and Jane Seymour, where a Man manifests his mind to go back in time to find and meet the woman he will fall in love with. In Clint's case, he must go back to the future, which is actually the past, and locate Kim his wife, somehow without interrupting the past, present for future. Knowing without a doubt, he loves her, and she loves him already. Clint thought about how this could be done, and how can he find a way back to the woman he loves, and his son Luke. Then Clint understood one thing at that moment, to have any chance of his return, the day must be won.)

Ok, Chloe my girl, let's not keep your mom waiting too long.

"Yeah Dad, It's Time to Clean the Fucking Dojo!"

Exactly Chlo!

Irish Warrior, what's the Hive Queen up to right now.

"Clint, she is on the move, and is walking towards the Radio Station Building alone, none of her DA soldiers are moving with her, almost as if they were ordered to stay back."

Crazy shit Irish,

Ok Burendo Warriors look alive, and stay alive, because Hive Queen is up to more of her evil ways of manipulation, and evil strategies. I guess we are about to find out something because she is about to speak, and now it looks like her DA soldiers have moved back with her and are standing directly behind their Queen.

"Dad this announcement Hive Queen is about to make is going to be about the evil I'm sensing that is en route to earth as we speak. This is going to solidify my fears, it means Hive Queen knows what this is, and this evil force is not on our side in anyway. You see dad, in all of my time traveling I have done throughout the world. I could only go back in time where human life was sustainable and existed. Also, I could only go forward in time, up until the year 2087 September 31t, which was the final day of human existence, meaning the earth was no longer sustainable for human life, so humankind no longer existed. It was horrific, and I barely made it back from that time with my life."

I hear what you are saying Chlo, and wow it took the Aliens from September 2026 to September 2087 to complete the extinction of the human race on Earth, so this is it, the final chance to save it all by ending this takeover now. I guess it must have pissed off the Hive Queen when I showed up the first time in 2026 and slowed the invasion process down. Although for these alien beasts, it wasn't 61 years in human time, it was one hour and one minute in the alien world. Ok, it looks and sounds like A-hole Hive Queen is speaking her bullshit now, so let's listen.

A-Hole Hive Queen

"This is all about to end for you Clint or shall I say, "The Man Called Clint", and your weak unprepared followers. No more human small talk, no more asking questions of me, and no more moments of conversations with a radio talk show host and pop tarts. You will soon understand that He knows and feels everything, nothing you can do will change your journey into death and suffering. There is nothing left for humans on planet Earth, other than fading away into the abyss. My King, my Lord, my Emperor is coming, and he will make you understand that human life on planet Earth is nothing but a dejected science experiment. Your time is over, my King is coming, and you are about to grapple with total power, and a force of evil on a level that your small human mind will not be able to grasp, I have nothing left to say, now you will have to face my Leader."

(The dark hateful sky slowly starts to brighten with a red ominous light of dreadful intentions breaking through the clouds is a very large-scale object that is generating massive power, and exact control as it floats in the sky.

The Man Called Clint, and his team look on with total amazement and shock. Suddenly this large disc-shaped object with numerous bright red illuminating lights attached to it becomes visible. Yes, aliens do exist, and they are more evil and vicious than anyone could have ever formulated in their mind. As the Alien spaceship floats silently in the air, a flash of dark light shoots out from beneath the undercarriage of this evil spaceship of death. A shadowless human form-like thing appears standing in front, and below the spacecraft. No fear or hesitation from this human-like form is present, because the Emperor of Evil has arrived and is ready to speak on the matter of humans, death, suffering, and pain. This is the final contact and the final conflict for the human race, the odds of survival are zero now, and they will soon discover why they are the prey and not the predator.)

Extinction Has Arrived

"Clint, this isn't good, whoever or whatever this leader of the alien race could be, it is showing no fear or worry about being separated from its battle army of DA(s), along with the Hive Queen. They have moved back away from the building again, and appear to be giving this Alien Leader some space, almost as if they are frightened of him."

You are right, he is creeping us out, along with his own army of DA(s). He must be their Lord of sorts, so maybe they are showing him respect or they are just totally afraid. Out of sight out of mind kind of thing, but he is here, so too late for that to occur.

Olivia, run a life scan on this Alien King and see what comes back on this strange abomination walking our way. Also, run a check in that spacecraft, I want to see if there are any more life forms inside.

"Yes Sensei, running it on both as we speak, it should come back in a couple seconds. Ok, the Spacecraft, does have some type of life form inside it still. The readout doesn't determine what it could be, but it does indicate a tremendous adrenaline source coming from whatever it could be inside the spacecraft. Now this Alien leader is a different story, it isn't alive, but isn't dead either."

Really Olivia, then what the shit sandwich is this medieval looking being.

"Sensei it's immortal! Meaning in the simplest terms, it can live forever."

"Great Clint, that damn Alien Ruler has better technology than us, and it's immortal. What are the chances."

Irish, you mean like Highlander!

"No Clint! Not like the fucking 1986 Highlander movie, plus I don't think this Alien leader is a Scottish swordsman, but then again, he does look a bit medieval."

I know Irish, we definitely just got dealt the jackass card, but let's play out the hand we got.

Chloe what's your take on this whole thing.

"Well Dad, this alien guy is dressed in an interesting type of armor, it looks traditional but has non-traditional characteristics. Based on what I'm observing, I believe this armor is similar to mine. Meaning, it can adapt, and change based on the threat or environment the wearer encounters. If it is similar, this means time travel is on the table, because I obtained my armor back in the medieval age. I am also getting a massive sense of evil, hate, and uncontrollable confidence coming from his presence. Just a thought, but either way we need to end him."

Most definitely Chlo, by the way where's your Dragon Yosai?

"Oh, he is on the roof of the Beaver County Radio station, just keeping watch like a gargoyle warding off evil spirits. When I attack, my flying winged fortress will also attack."

Really cool Chlo, you upgraded from dogs to a Dragon.

"Yep Dad, believe it or not a dragon is a lot like a dog, if it's a good dog that you treat well, it will give back its loyalty, and love with out hesitation. Although with a Dragon, you need to earn this in a very dangerous way, which is another tale for another day. "

Ok, Chloe, it soon will be time for the Silver Samurai to wield her sword, so save that story for another day. I would love to hear all about your quests.

"Absolutely Dad, I will definitely tell you that story one day. Now I have to tell you this, my armor is changing into full combat mode. Along with me, my armor must sense the complete darkness of evil that is walking up the concrete parking lot toward our destination. This is evil on a level that is human, supernatural, and alien in nature, if that makes any kind of sense. Why that is the case, I don't have an answer."

Well, I am sure we will find out in the next several minutes Chlo.

Sandra, and Olivia, how is the guy that was cured that survived the punishment from the DA(s), by any chance is he able to fight.

"Well Sensei, for what ever reason, he is sleeping, and won't wake up. The take over by one of those savage DA's must be exhausting mentally, and physically. "

Let him sleep Olivia, maybe when he wakes up, this will be all over.

Ok, everyone, this is the final battle, so fight with everything you have left in the tank. We make our stand here, and now. Once this Clown ass King Alien gets done with his speech, which I know he will probably make, based on past bullshit speeches, I got from Hive Queen. The chances are pretty good there will be one from the King Alien. When this speech is over, we attack with ultimate combat action, you must fight until your last breath, and until your heart no longer beats. Win the day, and save humanity.

"Clint, the Alien King dipshit is walking slowly towards the building and doesn't seem concerned at all to take cover or shield himself in any way. I mean that takes gigantic Alien balls to just walk up to the front door of your enemy, knowing we will fight to death."

Yea Irish, especially when the rest of his alien shithead force, including Hive Queen is just on the outskirts wondering, and waiting for things to unfold.

Ok everyone, be ready because the Dill Weed King is standing right in front of the building. He looks to be waiting for me to come outside and talk to him.

Stand fast Warriors, because I'm going outside to meet this King of the aliens, and I have no doubt there will be blood spilled on this day, and it will be the Alien King's blood. I have my trusty Han'i Ha, with three blade ranges of death with me to start the festivities. Here goes everything, time to hear what this Dill-Weed King has to say, either way, it's going to end in a very horrific way. Everyone stay inside, including you Chlo, I need to face the leader of this alien race alone for a moment, and more than likely we will be told by this Alien Leader to lay down our souls, and just give up. Also, Chlo, or should I say the Silver Samurai, keep your Dragon Yosai ready to defend, because when it starts it will happen fast, and reaction time must be precise.

Burendo Warriors stay focused, and be prepared, Irish Warrior, I know you got my back.

(With no hesitation, and solid focus, the Man Called Clint, steps outside to meet the Emperor of an Alien race, while everyone watches, including the Hive Queen, and her DA Soldiers. What happens next, no one could have ever predicted, because this Emperor Alien King is like nothing ever encountered in this world or any universe for matter.

Survival of the species is cruel, unpredictable, real, and without remorse, so the Man Called Clint must embrace the certitude that what he is about to face is evil on full display. As Clint stands outside the doors of the Beaver County Radio Station, he senses this Emperor Alien King is preparing to pull back the veil of evil and release a wrath of bloodlust, until his thirst is satisfied. The duel has begun, and the Emperor Alien King begins to speak and starts with a bloodcurdling laugh of sorts, followed by a humorous comment, Clint decides at that very moment to just listen and observe.)

Emperor Alien King

The Final Hunt Has Commenced!

"Good evening, I was wondering, do you have any more Pop Tarts left because they really smelled delicious. Almost as delicious as human flesh and blood to me. You see, I do find amazing interest in the different foods your species enjoy feeding on. Humans for the most part step outside the box with unusual menu items. I know you are wondering with complete astonishment how I know about the Pop Tarts, which was Eddy Crow's last meal request. You see, I will tell you a little secret about my species, or shall I say Dead Adrenaline(s), as you are so affectionally named them. When our kind consumes or even bites, some of the knowledge that a particular human possess is transferred into the DA. Then I remove this knowledge from the DA, by way of a form of alien telepathy. Mind to mind if you will indulge me, you see every single human, dead or even alive that my DA(s) have eaten, or even just chomped on are affected by this. Any past or present knowledge is taken, and they don't even know it even if they survived the attack. Now on a very exciting side of this knowledge-gathering quest, if one of my DAs takes over a human subject's body, and mind completely, then past, present, and future knowledge is obtained totally. Contained in all of this human data is pain, guilt, sadness, happiness, hate, moral, and immoral thoughts or memories.

Lastly, which is a very interesting, but is a non-useful emotion "**LOVE**". You humans show love, which is very ambiguous feeling, you love money, places, things, yourself, and others. And some absolute forms of love, it is what you call true love, which explains the weakness of your species. You see, from your past experiences with my DA(s), you might have thought they were sad or happy, as they fed on your kind, or maybe you thought they were upset, because their mother was losing in the battle to take over planet earth at times. When I say mother, I'm talking about the Hive Queen, which you so arrogantly named her. She is one of my Queens, so I will let that one slide, but back to the emotions of sad or happy DA(s). It was neither of these emotions, they were feeling, it was fear that I, the Emperor would show up on earth to end this invasion permanently. They feared that no one will be left alive, including my own kind. I'm a very busy Emperor, and I don't have the time to monitor, a pathetic simple annihilation of a planet. See, I have traveled the universe, and have continuously gathered knowledge. All of the species I have encountered have many differences, and many similarities, but they have one thing in common. They all can be killed, in one form or another, this brings me great pleasure, which makes this endeavor worth my time.

Up to this point, you have seen violence on a massive level, and have been told by my Queen that we have come to planet Earth to take it over and make planet earth our new home. Only some of that is true, you see my Queen has a tendency to tell lies, meaning just about everything she told you about us was made up for effect. I guess she enjoys it, but it serves no purpose when the real reasons we here are simple. Killing other species is exciting, and very pleasurable. The gathering of knowledge is a bonus, but the blood-fest is totally worth the hunt. Yes, I said hunt, destroy, and consume everything down to the knowledge of that species. Now that you know our little secret, my name is Vlad, and from what I have gathered, your name is Clint, or shall I say, "The Man Called Clint", and no I don't. want to hear you speak, because what I'm about to unleash will be like nothing you have ever seen before or will ever see again."

"Let's start with my name, I am known as Emperor Vlad, which is true, but I go by many names, which usually change based on the host body I invade. I have what you humans call a spaceship, spacecraft, or UFO, and yes, I

209

do prefer to travel by ship, instead of what you like to call a light sphere, which is actually what we look like without a human, animal or creature shell host. I have the ability to time travel, which has taken me all over the universe.

I have been to the past, present and future, so my knowledge gathering has been exceptional. But on this day, I will obtain a most extraordinary gathering of knowledge, along with the blood and flesh of you and your followers, including the Silver Samurai, and her Dragon. After this deed is done, I will continue my wrath, and leave Beaver County, PA, only to continue my hunt. You see, I kill every living species on this planet and leave extinction behind. Now that you and your followers know what is about to befall, I have one more gift of knowledge to offer you, before I commence with the hunt. My name is Vlad, and I'm the Emperor of my species, but I go by another. A name you will know Clint, a name that will make you understand what is about to happen. My name is Vlad the Impaler, born in Sighisoara, Transylvania, and ruled in 15th century Europe, my methods of destroying my enemy are vast. You see Clint, I traveled to the 15th Century Europe in the year 1476 and located Vlad. He was evil, powerful, unrelentingly, and craved death and violence on a gigantic level. I respected this and knew at that very moment, I would take his mind and body as a permanent host. One would think, his will to survive would not make him an easy takeover, but it was the opposite. Vlad The Impaler embraced the opportunity to become greater and more evil, so he willfully except my Alien entity into his soul. In the year 1476 *Vlad the Impaler* was documented in historical records as the year he died, but don't you see evil never really dies,

Vlad the Impaler, became Emperor Vlad on that day, and evolution took over. I control, him, but he is part of my genetic makeup, and now his evil is my evil, and my evil is

210

his evil. I do have one more thing that must be mentioned and shown before the hunt begins. Vlad goes by one other name, and this name will make you understand what is coming. **Dracula!** And just so you aren't wondering, yes, he is now an **Alien-Vampire!"** Prepare for the wrath of evil, the time of humans is over, I will give you a few minutes to realize I am death, and life cannot exist in the realm of death, and then the hunt will commence."

Ok, Burendo Shotokan Warriors come outside, and take your position. Spread out and keep alert, this is it.

Irish where's my daughter the Silver Samurai.

"Oh, she's already exited the building and is sitting on Yosai, on top of the roof. Clint, this is some really scary fucked up shit. Vlad The Impaler, who is a Dracula, and an Alien Emperor blended (Burendo) together into one complete package of Mid evil-Nosferatu-Extraterrestrial origin, which is really messed up shit. I guess Vlad The Impaler, really did drink blood.

You are so right Irish Warrior, but if we survive this, I wouldn't mind watching the 1922 silent German film, Nosferatu: Symphony of Horror, or at least watch the iconic scene where Count. Orlok ascends a staircase in a shadowy form. Anyways, by the way, that was very nice Nosferatu usage in describing Count Vlad Dill-Weed.

"Clint if this is the end, remember you have always been a top shelf friend, but you have issues."

Right back at you Irish.

Burendo Shotokan Warriors, It's Time to Clean Fucking Dojo, one last time! Count Vlad Dill-Weed has just returned, and that is one ugly ass Alien-Vampire. What a hideous sight to behold!

Chloe! You ready to launch.

"Yeah, Dad! The Silver Samurai and her trusty Dragon Yosai are ready and prepared to face death."

I hope so for everyone's sake, because **death just arrived, and it's got fangs!!**

"DEATH JUST ARRIVED, AND IT'S GOT FANGS"

<u>General Acknowledgments & References/comments
Made in this book have been inspired by.</u>

<u>Movie Titles</u>

Sturges.J(Director). (1960). The Magnificent Seven *[Film].*
Production Companies: The Mirisch Company, Alpha
Productions. Starring Yul Brynner, Steve McQueen, James
Coburn, Charles Bronson, Robert Vaugh, Brad Dexter,
Horst Buchholz.

Kurosawa's. A(Director). (1954). Seven
Samurai.Japanese[Film]. *Production Company: Toho.*

Shyamalan M. N(Director). (1999). The Sixth Sense [Film].
Production Company: Hollywood Pictures, Spyglass
Entertainment, The Kennedy /Marshall Company, Barry
Mendel Productions.
Starring Bruce Willis.

Pal.G(Director). (1960). The Time Machine [Film].
Production Company: Metro-Goldwyn-Mayer, Galaxy
Films.Starring Rod Taylor.

Hyams. P. (Director). (2005). A Sound of Thunder [Film].
Production Company: Franchise Pictures, Crusader
Entertainment, Baldwin Entertainment Group, Etic Films,
Forge, QI Quality International. Starring Catherine
McCorma, Ben Kingsley, and Edward Burns.

Fleischer. R. (Director). (1973) Soylent Green [Film].
Production Company: Walter Thacher- Walter Seltzer.
Starring Charlton Heston.

Sagal B. (Director). (1971) Omega Man [Film]. Production Company: Walter Seltzer Productions. Starring Charlton Heston.

Scott R. (Director). (1979) Alien [Film]. Production Companies: 20 Century-Fox, Brandywine Productions. Starring Sigourney Weaver.

Cameron J. (Director). (1986) Aliens [Film]. Production Company: Brandywine Productions. Starring Sigourney Weaver.

Stallone S. (Director). (1985) Rocky IV [Film]. Production Companies: United Artist, ChartOff Winkler Productions. Starring Sylvester Stallone.

Cosmatos, G. P. (Director). (1986) Cobra [Film]. Production Company: The Cannon Group. Starring Sylvester Stallone.

Kotcheff T. (Director). (1982) First Blood, Rambo [Film]. Production Companies: The Wallis Interactive, Carolco Pictures, Anabasis Investments, N.V. Starring Sylvester Stallone.

Zemeckis R. (Director). (1985) *Back to the Future [Film]. Production Company:* Starring Michael J. Fox.

Cameron J. (Director). (1989) The Abyss [Film]. Production Company: 20 Century Fox. Starring Ed Harris, Mary Elizabeth Mastrantonio, and Michael Biehn.

Maylam T. (Director). (1992) Split Second [Film]. Production Company: Muse Productions, Challenge Films. Starring Rutger Hauer and Kim Cattrall

Cohen R. (Director). (1996) Dragon Heart [Film]. Distributed by Universal Pictures. Starring Dennis Quad, Draco the Dragon voiced by Sean Connery.

Romero G. (Director). (1968) *Night of Living Dead [Film]*. *Production Company: Image Ten.*

.

Kiersch F. (Director). (1984) Children of the Corn. [Film]. Production Companies: Angeles Entertainment Group, Cinema Group, Hal Roach Studios, Inverness Productions, Planet Productions.

Spielberg S. (Director). (1981) Raiders of the Lost Ark [Film]. Productions Companies: Lucas Film LTD. Starring Harrison Ford.

Hodges M. (Director) (1980) Flash Gordon [Film]. Production Companies: Starling Productions, Famous Films. Starring Sam J. Jones.

Fincher D. (Director). (2008) The Curious Case of Benjamin Button [Film]. Production Companies: Paramount Pictures, Warner Bros Pictures, The Kennedy / Marshall Company. Starring Brad Pitt.

Szwarc J. (Director). (1980) Somewhere in Time [Film]. Production Company: Rastar. Starring Christopher Reeve and Jane Seymour.

Hill W.(Director). (1982) 48 Hrs.[Film]. Production Company: Lawrence Gordon productions. Starring Nick Nolte and Eddy Murphy.

Reitman I.(Director).(1984). Ghost Busters[Film]. Production Companies: Columbia- Delphi Productions, Black Rhino. Starring Harold Ramis, Bill Murray, Dan Aykroyd, Ernie Hudson and Sigourney Weaver.

Murnau F.W. (Director). (1922) Nosferatu: Symphony of Horror [Silent Film]. Production Company: Prana Film.

Kldiashvili N. (Director). (1975) Rikki-Tikki-Tavi [Animated Film].

Mulcahy R. (Director). (1986) Highlander [Film]. Production Company: Thorn EMI Screen Entertainment, Highlander Productions, Davis-Panzer Productions.
Starring Christopher Lambert, Sean Connery, Roxanne Hart, Clancy Brown.

Miscellaneous Source / Book Titles

Dead Adrenaline: One Man's Journey To Survive Beaver County, PA. (Published June 2023), Written by Clinton J. Kurtyka.

The Bible.

George Orwell: Writer of the Nineteen Eighty-Four Novel.

"Do not go gentle into that good night"(Written by Welsh Poet and writer Dylan Marlais Thomas.)

(Han'i Ha) Han'i: Means selected range, and Ha: Means the tempered cutting edge of a blade in Japanese. Han'i Ha (Range Blade) is a fictional sword in Dead Adrenaline series.

Special Thanks

Eddy Crow / Talk show host / radio personality on Beaver County Radio. Thank you for giving me permission to use your name, personality, and likeness in the book Time Break Expedition, The Return Dead Adrenaline II. The Eddy Crow character in this book is one of a kind.

Television shows / series

Six Million Dollar Man television series (1973-1978)
Honorable acknowledgment

American singer and actor, Elvis Presley (1935-1977).
Nicknamed "King of Rock and Roll."

Historical acknowledgment

Haja-no-Ontachi (Great-Evil-Crushing Blade)

This sword is the longest sword in Japan and was donated to the Hanaoka Hachiman shrine in 1859.

Vlad the Impaler was an evil, brutal ruler in Wallachian history, whose cruel methods of punishing his enemies gained notoriety in 15th century Europe.

<u>Acknowledgment of Mythological, & Fictional Characters,</u>
<u>along with the Excalibur sword from many countless</u>
<u>movies and books.</u>

King Arthur, and the Knights of the Round Table,
Excalibur Sword, and Merlin Ambrosius & The
Lady of the Lake.

Dracula is a character from many books and movies,
some scholars do believe that
this evil character was derived from the historical
Wallachian prince (Vlad the Impaler.)

<u>Honorable Mention and acknowledgment</u>

New Brighton Car Cruise Beaver County, PA.1985present.

Hot Wheels (Mattel)

Pop Tarts (Kellanova, formerly Kellogg's).

<u>Musical band name, Song titles, Performer and</u>
<u>Soundtrack.</u>

1986 release, Album (The Final Countdown), by the
Swedish rock band Europe.

The Busboys, sang the song, (The Boys Are Back In
Town) for the movie 48 Hrs in 1982. Also the song
(Cleaning Up The Town)for the movie GhostBusters in
1984.

219

Special thanks to each of these businesses.

Business/ Sign or Logo used by verbal, and written permission.

Victoria's Embroidering, 464 Deer Ln, Rochester, PA 15074. Phone:724-728-3484
Info@victoriasembroidering.com
(Victoria's Embroidering)
Follow-On Facebook (Victorias Embroidering).
victoriasembroidering.com
Instagram victoriasembroidery (@victoriasembroidery).

Coffee Beanery, 1466 Old Brodhead Rd, Monaca, PA 15061. Phone: 878-207-2385.
Email:72@coffeebeanery.com
(Coffee Beanery Monaca).
Follow-on Facebook (Facebook.com /
CoffeeBeaneryMonaca)
Instagram (Coffee- Beanery- Monaca).

The Little Green Bookstore, 104 N Main St, Zelienople, PA 16063.Phone: 724-473-4599.
(The Little Green Bookstore).
Follow-on Facebook (The Little Green Bookstore)
Instagram (littlegreenbookstore). bookshop.org/shop/
littlegreenbookstore libro.fm/littlegreenbookstore

Zirat Auto Electric Services, 3308 Sunflower Rd, New Brighton, PA 15066.Phone: 724-846-7690.
(Zirat's Auto Electric Services).

Health Hut-Chippewa, : 110 McMillen Ave, Beaver Falls, PA 15010. Phone: 724-843-3625. HealthHutStores.com. **(Health Hut).**
Follow-on Facebook (Health Hut Tribe) & Instagram(@shophealthhut).

Health Hut-2-Beaver, 1617 3rd St, Beaver, PA 15009. Phone: 724- 770-0711.

All Hazard Tactical.
(ALL HAZARD TACTICAL).
http:www.allhazardstactical.com
Follow-On Facebook(@allhazardstactical) & Instagram(@allhazardstactical).

Beaver County Radio, WBVP, WMBA & 99.3 FM. 4301 Dutch Ridge Road Beaver, PA 15009.
Business Phone:724-846-4100, Talk Shows/Request: 724-774-1888 or 724-843-1388. Email: bcr@beavercountyradio.com **(Beaver County Radio).**
Follow-On Facebook (WBVP WMBA, Beaver County Radio)
Instagram (Beaver CountyRadio) (@beavercountyradio).

Websites:

www.wikipedia.org
www.lmdp.com
https//:blackbeltwiki.com

Text Editing

Kitty Hogan, Clinton J. Kurtyka and Grant A. Miller

Images:

Art Design and Photographs of the front of book cover for Time Break Expedition, The Return Dead Adrenaline II novel were completed by Clinton J. Kurtyka.

The back cover of book was created by AI(Artificial Intelligence)

All drawings and artwork contained within this book (Dead Adrenaline II) were completed by Clinton J. Kurtyka, with exceptions of all AI images.

Photograph and photo artwork modifications contained within this book (Dead Adrenaline II) were taken and completed by Clinton J. Kurtyka. Some of the images were created by AI, and did have slight modifications completed by Clinton J. Kurtyka.

Shotokan Karate, Taekwondo-o, Hapkido, Aikido,Judo, and other Martial Arts sources. Japanese & Korean Terminology.

One Strike Karate (Burendo Shotokan) Handbook, Written & Compiled by: Grant Miller & Clinton J. Kurtyka. 08/31/2020- revised formerly "Ichigeki Karate"- This handbook supersedes all previous ones.

Miller, Grant A. The Hapkido Way, Publications by GAMiller Consulting P.C. 2016. Miller, Grant A. The Secret Origins of Aiki- Jujutsu. Publication by GAMiller Consulting P.C. 2016.

*Photograph owned by One Strike Karate (Burendo Shotokan). Courtesy of One Strike Karate.One Strike Karate (Burendo Shotokan) school was established in 2005 by Master Grant Miller.The Dojo is open for business and is operated by Head Instructor Master Clint Kurtyka at 1299 Pennsylvania Ave. Monaca, PA.15061.

Death Has Many Names!

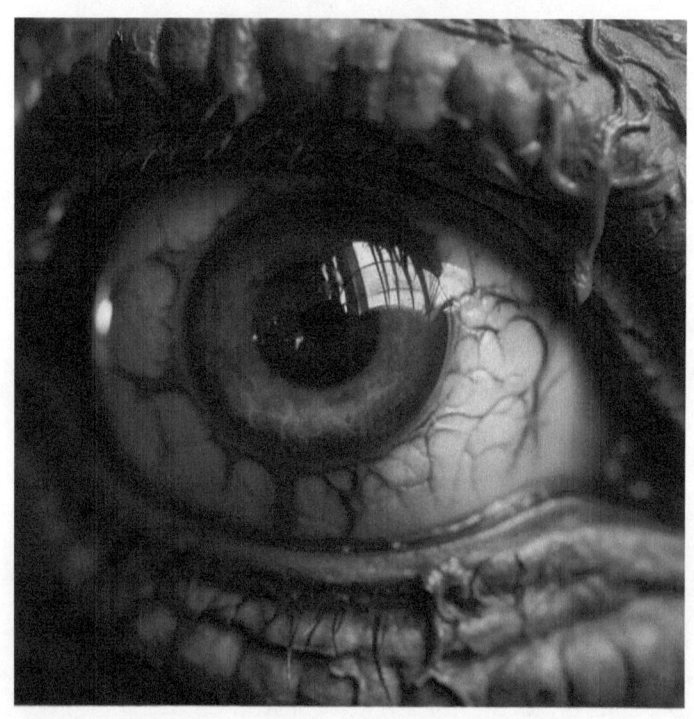

The End

About Author

Clinton J. Kurtyka was born in Beaver County, Pennsylvanian, and has work in Law Enforcement in Pennsylvania for over 29 years. Also, Clinton operates a Karate school called One Strike Karate (Burendo Shotokan) in Monaca, Pennsylvania. Growing up in the Beaver County area as a youth, Clinton always had a love for special effects, movies, and great stories. Science-Fiction Horror, Fantasy, and Action Adventure were genres that intrigued and fueled his interest. Based on his experiences in Law Enforcement, long-term knowledge of martial arts, and interest in story telling. Clinton decided to write his first ever book, which was completed in June 2023. The book was called Dead Adrenaline: One Man's Journey To Survive Beaver County, PA. This book was the first installment of the Dead Adrenaline series, and now Clinton has completed the second book in the series, which is called Time Break Expedition, The Return Dead Adrenaline II. Dead Adrenaline II is a continuation of Science Fiction-Horror ride that took readers on a voyage into the abyss the first time, so find a safe seat, sit back and enjoy the 2nd installment of the Dead Adrenaline series.

Available on Amazon!
Murder At Witches'Hollow (Detective Shiokawa Murder Mysteries)

by (Grant A. Miller)

Over 125 years ago three witches were burned alive in a small rural community in western Pennsylvania. In the present day, a planned vacation for Detective Shiokawa to visit his friend turns into an intriguing murder mystery where his insight and knowledge is needed to help bring the killer to justice. Difficulties abound as he is engulfed between natural and supernatural forces at play which lead to intriguing individuals, circumstances and dangers. Shiokawa must use all his experience to help navigate the pathways and find out what happens when there is a murder in witches' hollow.

Available on Amazon!
(Struggle of Temptation) by Chere Lynn)

Ever since, Sara Gibson, was a little girl, she dreamed of becoming one of the most
successful directors in Hollywood. Her unconventional method of directing insured her to be the most sought-after director of her time.

As ambition drove her to the top, she kept relationships at a distance. They proved to be obscure. Most men were intimidated by her drive and success.

Rob Donavan, newcomer to the acting world, captured the role of a lifetime, under the direction of Miss Gibson. Could he also capture her heart with his charming demeanor?

Available on Amazon

(Ravenscythe by Beth Ann Flowers & Grant A. Miller)

The ghosts Granite and Batty have haunted the castle for hundreds of years, and with its conversion five-star rated hotel, the fun has only just begun! Join them as they embark on a mystery that involves ghosts, vampires, and gargoyles, oh my! The pamphlet for the hotel reads: "Welcome to the Royal Ravenscythe Hotel! Enjoy this historic castle with its original antique furniture and art. The hotel has updated amenities with your comfort in mind! We spared no expense with our gym, indoor pool, gourmet meals at our restaurant, a lively pub, beautiful flower and herb gardens, a maze with a wishing well in the center, and lots more!" The 'lots more' is where the excitement begins. Join them on this adventure!

**The Adventure Continues and the Past, Present, and
Future will Never be the same!**

Coming Soon!

**The third installment of the Dead Adrenaline series,
the battle for good vs evil continues.**

"Don't Be A Dill-Weed"

www.ingramcontent.com/pod-product-compliance
Lightning Source LLC
Chambersburg PA
CBHW031100020726
47495CB00007B/1971